KARLOFF'S
CIRCUS

KARLOFF'S CIRCUS
ACCOMPLICE 4

STEVE AYLETT

Copyright © Steve Aylett 2004

The right of Steve Aylett to be identified as the author
of this work has been asserted by him in accordance with
the Copyright, Designs and Patents Act 1988.

First published in Great Britain in 2004 by

Gollancz
An imprint of the Orion Publishing Group
Orion House, 5 Upper St Martin's Lane, London WC2H 9EA

This mass-market paperback edition first published in 2005

A CIP catalogue record for this book is available
from the British Library

ISBN 0 575 07625 9

Printed in Great Britain by
Clays Ltd, St Ives plc

hello Mum

www.orionbooks.co.uk

for Dad

Steve Aylett is author of *The Crime Studio,*
Bigot Hall, Slaughtermatic, The Inflatable Volunteer,
Toxicology, Atom, Shamanspace, Only an Alligator,
The Velocity Gospel and *Dummyland.*

www.steveaylett.com

'I'm expected to sleep in a diving mask and false beard. The priesthood is not what I had hoped.'

– Bingo Violaine,
Hand It To Sparky

1

Hanging on a Star

Friends don't shake hands

Suicide is a permanent solution to an ever-replenishing series of temporary problems, but Mike Abblatia was concerned only with the immediate one concerning his business. Every day, cars were stolen from the garage where he worked. Now he walked across Jericho Bridge away from Accomplice, the only town capable of being complicated by laziness. Some believed property was theft and others believed they were renting. But while they led a life of Sundays, Abblatia had been living an extra day between Thursday and Friday, growing a little older than his years. His back was killing him. Halfway across the bridge, he climbed into the black suspension girders and stood a while listening to the sizzle of night insects. Then he let himself fall, accelerating toward the soupy river. Air rushed up his shirtsleeves.

His back split, turning open like a time-lapse flower. Sticky wings were blown into use and filled, shuddering. The slippery current of the water began to blur past his sixteen-hole boots.

Behind his flight a heavy train roared across the bridge.

In the cab of the train, smoke blasting past his pointed face, Karloff Velocet stood like a sentry to himself. A silver-painted midget had already capered through Accomplice slapping up posters which declared CONSIDER THIS YOUR NEW MOTHER beneath the face of a jet-eyed fright with marshmallow flesh. All recognised the depicted creature as a Karloff clown and fear had gripped the populace. Karloff's company travelled in a train which tended to arrive by bursting out of someone's mouth and everyone was alarmed that they might become the winner of this terminal lottery. Even as Barny Juno approached his parents' shack with an insect, the etheric-buffered locomotive was shrieking toward the town. But then Karloff happened to glimpse a fan of white wings erupting away from the bridge, gliding low and fast through the gloom. Without emotion he reached aside and jerked the emergency stop.

Barny Juno climbed in through the rear window of the shack, landing lightly so as not to waken his dozing mother. He approached the spartan canary cage with a katydid in his hand. The insect resembled fairly closely the pet which he had accidentally killed on his last visit. His parents would assume the memory of Lovely Ramone's death was the sort of crappy hallucination common to codgers like them. As he tipped the bug into the cage he heard his father squelching around on the porch. The boards were steeped in swamp water.

'Well look who it ain't,' said Pa Juno as Barny emerged into the night. 'Lightning in a cot.' He looked at Barny from beneath a writing chaos of bioluminescent hair.

'I came to give you all the news that's fit to tell.'

'Brought a paper?'

'No.'

'Even there you fail. Me and your mother are coming into West Coum for the blood levy soon, I need to know what's happening. You want me to be a laughing stock, a country bumpkin? For all I know they're wearing iron trousers over there and I'll be the only one in these stupid ones made of mahogany.'

'Well that reminds me of one piece of news – doomed Eddie Gallo is trying to extend the flyover on his own by quietly hammering bits of timber to the end.'

'Quietly hammering? Sounds like he's just horsing around.'

'And Kenny Reactor's started growing arses over at the allotments.'

'As if those buttock cobblestones to the west aren't enough to damn us all.'

'Also the cannon people are shouting about guns a lot. What is a gun, Father?'

'It was a method of moving lead quickly from one place to another.'

'Like a pencil?'

'And aluminium.'

'Like a pen?'

'They were used to force people to do things.'

'To put down what people have to do?'

'Swiftly and utterly.'

'That doesn't sound so bad.'

Barny saw something white flashing through the trees. Some sort of angel was beating through the mushy brush like an injured swan, followed by a load of shambling circus freaks trailing orange plastic nets.

'I'm glad we're on the same page with this thing,' his father told him, rolling a cigarette. 'For once you're not away in your crazy fantasy world.'

'There's a bunch of circus freaks chasing some sort of angel through the forest.'

'There you go again.'

'I mean it, Father.'

'Don't call me that,' Pa Juno snapped.

Barny was pointing at the clotted waterways when the door banged open and Ma Juno hung out wailing, 'My innocent boy eaten by a monster!'

'I'm all right, Mother,' Barny assured her.

Ma Juno wept that her 'innocent boy' was a tiny fruitfly which she and Pa Juno kept in the canary cage. Now someone of precocious cruelty had flicked a katydid in there and the fly had approached it all eager and aglow, fooled by the bigger bug's fruit-like camouflage. 'Think of poor Ryan's terror when the slice of apple opened up like a Swiss army knife,' she sobbed. 'Evil!'

'I'm not evil,' Barny protested. 'What about the bug in there? I took care of it.'

Pa Juno enfolded his wife, regarding Barny in disgust and affront. 'You took care of it all right.'

In the town square the following day there was a good deal of irresponsibility and a good deal that made sense. Barny entered the square riding on a cow. He had met the mammal in a field and it had looked utterly bored. Now he rode toward his friends Gregor and Edgy, who were standing idle outside the Ultimatum Restaurant. 'Why are you riding that cow around, Bubba?' asked Edgy.

'The lion's in a funny mood.'

'So is the Round One here,' said Edgy, pointing to his oval associate. 'He's been looking at his own reflection in this window for two hours.'

'His gob's a bit glossy,' Barny observed.

'That's human saliva,' Edgy told him, 'the final proof that he's not a mere golem like the papers keep saying.' He turned to Gregor. 'You're not doing yourself any favours with this window-staring, Round One. What's on your mind?'

And Gregor seemed to blow a head gasket, springing at the glass hips first and smashing the whole thing down. Barny knew enough to wheel the cow away at once, strolling it towards the crowd which had gathered to watch Rod Jayrod, jug-eared master of the Cannon Sect, mount a powder barrel to deliver a diatribe. Barny heard Edgy shouting chidingly, 'Hey, will you stop it?' and other yelling from bystanders outside the restaurant.

'Glory in the spectacle of this fellow, Mrs Cow,' said Barny, and they stopped to watch the Fusemaster in his black and blue vestments, two fuseheads on either side of him swinging red dust from sanctified powder pouches.

'In the words of the philosopher Bingo Violaine,' Jayrod declared, ' "Truth isn't beguiled, people are. Truth remains whether anyone's gazing that way or not. It's the most patient thing in the world." We seek the return of our rightful property, the Wesley Kern gun, the *objet ballistique*, that portable expression of the inner cannon which is spoken of in myth and legend.' He flourished a fossilised cheese sandwich. 'We offer this remnant as reward for information leading to the reclamation of the Kern gun and its restoration to our shrine. Can you do any less than fill the absence on our altar?' He then began chanting to drown out any reply which might ruffle his question, finally droning it down into silence. 'That lovely chant is beyond your understanding.'

'Your ideas have been grown like a translation, no wonder!' shouted someone.

'Shut your face!' snapped the priest.

'You probably heard someone talking about his passionate devotion to something or other and in a state of high chin and jealousy swore your life to a busted cannonball which happened to be the first stupid thing you saw lying about the gaff!'

'Silence! Nothing can influence me, ladies and gentlemen,' Jayrod declared archly. 'I'm as loose as a flag.'

As his mouth was open to say 'flag', a steam train came bellowing out of it, about which his head expanded and snapped like a rubber band. His body was obliterated under the carve of wheels and machinery as the enamelled engine screeched across the tarmac, rocketing through the front of Snorters Café and bunching to a stop in a boom of steam and earth. The train had come to rest in a zigzag pattern and the scattered crowd closed in again hesitantly, slipping in goofer fuel.

Karloff Velocet shot from the smoke stack and cartwheeled to a carriage roof in the thick of his audience. His clothing appeared to have been carved from wax. He was striped up and down like a humbug. His neck was constricted by a blue ruff which resembled a giant human iris. And most dismal of all, he wore a glass top hat which was a barber's shop pole, its red and white turn spiralling ever upward. The assembly roared with impatience.

'Structure applause around my temporary stance, everyone!' Karloff cried. 'I bring to you all the disadvantages of bloody mayhem! Parlour tricks which have escaped my control! Shabby secrets ejected and at large! Ballerinas to shock and appal you! Scalped clowns dipped in dove paint! Resentful rarees and pointless oddities! Barbaric skull percussionists and bandaged fire bugs! "I'm leaving here and don't care," you may tell yourself, but you crackers and yokels will experience the spectacle of hectic endeavour! We dangle into your landscape, as if asked! We're desperate men! There – I've said it! Old capers turn me on! In fact everything else is just pants! I realise that my constant proximity to such events may make it difficult for you to have any confidence in what I have to say. So feast your eyes. In fact I insist on it!'

Along the twisted rack of trailers carved with sigils and baffle-like creeper fluting, boilerplate doors flew off and a platoon of clowns surged into the square, bearing all the paraphernalia of their foul calling. Among them were freaks, tumblers, crumblers and flamers. The crowd screamed in disappointment. 'You expected dogs – now you understand!' cried Karloff Velocet. 'See the Killer Midgets, previously known as the Terror Midgets! The Evolutionist, the Liquid Acrobat, Big Bumperton the Hornblower, the Caged Angel, Manticore Terry, the Fatal Rhino, Sue Egypt, the Ermine Fraud, the Beast Man and Blitzer Twill! Ben Panthera, falcon-headed problem that won't go away! Jeffrey Jamar – answerable to no one! Nick Genie, speechless with drink! Mr Lipid, full of malice and anger – what a guy! Felix Kyro, who has killed until killing can reward him no longer! See the unexpected gasp for breath amid precious stones! The Operating Theatre of Flowers! The Tunnel of Hounds! The Cordial Perilous! The Hall of Mirrors – all flat and normal, for you are grotesque enough! And it's all nice and legal! Bring your gilly children and hear them scream as though snagged in a combine! Down with coincidence! Fugitive from the slowly converging bicycles of the dull – the Circus of the Heart's Shell! Check it out!'

'What's all this crap?' asked Barny, kicking a clown away.

'Karloff's stupid Circus,' said Edgy, his tufted head bobbing above the crowd. There prevails an unbroken harmony among those who enjoy strangling clowns. It is not merely the matter of remaining at large after the act, but the brotherhood created in the subtle comparison of pressure, bonecrush and pop-eyed expression. Edgy restricted the larynx of one now as he elaborated, 'You rescued the lion from them, remember?'

Barny remembered, and wheeled the cow slowly around to see Karloff entering the mayoral palace.

'Look at that cute little bug-eyed pig standing on its back trotters,' cooed the Mayor.

'That's a mirror, sir,' Dietrich pointed out.

Rudloe was shaken. 'That's it,' he said with dignity. 'The next happy smile will be a guest here.' From his high office like a birdcage he gazed down on the square, alerted by calliope music. 'There's a procession of two-ton carny trucks all joined up like an accordion down there. And a load of clowns wearing fright fatigues. That music! Ears are the window to the brain, they say. Horrible, horrible.' He sat at his desk and cradled his primary chin. Recently the Mayor had fractured his jaw while attempting a cocksure expression and he was determined not to over-exert it today. 'Don't like Velocet. Always jumping to the right conclusions.'

The demon Dietrich, who had defected from hell to listen

to this bullshit, nodded his anvil head. 'What I admire in a politician like yourself is not the intelligence you boast but the stupidity you hide beneath a bushel, Mister Mayor. As the philosopher Violaine said, "Blame an ant if you desire no repercussions."'

'You know who commissioned Violaine's statue? Violaine, a year before he died. He even specified the rock which was to be used. At this rate all *I'll* be leaving is the snot ejected by my final gasp.'

Karloff Velocet strode in unannounced, his hat spiralling and all. 'Don't kiss me, I've got a cold.'

'Very funny. Dietrich, this boiled twist of evil and chaos is Fall Marshall of the carny down there. Karloff, this totem of winged armour is Dietrich Hammerwire, my new campaign advisor.'

'A paravamp.' Karloff spun an imitation emerald cane topped by the shrunken head of a tailor. 'I forgot what a hub Accomplice is for transient demons. Attracted by the stink of failure – and prayer.'

'That's a lazy analysis,' said Dietrich.

'Why duplicate effort? Between demons and people, I'll curse people. Nothing's harder to exude than respect, eh Dietrich? Tends to come across as constipation. How do you pay it, Mayor? Him I mean. Mind if I sit down?'

'Dietrich eats the floor lobsters hereabouts. There's a knack. Tail first.'

'Convenient,' said Karloff, seating himself. 'I see you've added another floor to that multistorey chin of yours. Still in competition with doomed Eddie Gallo?'

'Yes. The brain nature provided him remains unclaimed in his skull. I doubt he knows of its existence. He's trying to rebuild the flyover with some sticks. Got a sliced turnip on his campaign posters. Not much of an enemy.'

'Yes, I think we can assume that the most exciting incidents in life occur *outside* a turnip. You know, Mayor, we're similar in many ways. Neither of us suffers fools gladly, and we both consider each other fools. I have pondered the matter and decided that you and I shall be friends.'

'And when will this feeling grip me? I have a busy schedule.'

'Oh?'

'I accept your tantalising until twelve thirty. Then – slam in the face. That loco vimana you arrived in is clearly creepchannel-shielded, a scarship. You issued from a labyrinth – not an auspicious beginning. Then you come in here wearing those mad, mad trousers and commence tugging my chops as if there were no tomorrow.'

'I'm sure I'd select a more fulfilling way to pass my final hours than tugging your chops, Mayor.'

'That's as may be. But the fact is every time you visit all hell rips loose.'

'Then why invite me?'

'My ex-advisor Max Gaffer invited you as a kiss-off when he quit – the chain of office sinks me in betrayal. Accomplice will have my guts.'

'Accomplice doesn't even know when or where it is. This locked peninsula, the Island of the Strong Door. How normal do you think *this* is?' Karloff gestured negligently back at the towering Dietrich, whose wings shivered in irritation.

The Mayor could see shadows moving beneath the question. 'One thing at a time.'

Karloff widened his eyes in mock outrage. 'Blasphemy.' He stood to leave. 'Come to our opening performance.' And he waved a hand at Dietrich. 'You must be at least this evil to enter.'

When he was gone, Dietrich suggested that Mayor Rudloe might want to 'get involved' in a folksy way. 'Hold the hanky in some dismal magic trick. Rescue a rodent from a hat. You'll be heaped with so much admiration your ribs'll stack down on each other, trapping nerves and so on. Your corrupt and bloated administration will continue apace.'

The Mayor let out a sigh. 'Why appease the millstone of my

constituents when I could so easily remove it? I've improved conditions quite a bit around here. Heads on an old wall, that soon changed. Surgical insect heaven – banned. But the moss'll be growing in my name before I'm appreciated. What's it all about, Dieter?'

'Greed, Mayor. In this sublunary world of yours, chaos is static or centrifugal. With this carny of Karloff's, better to be the centre of the storm.'

'I'm not sure I can recommend your audacious plan to the Conglomerate.'

'You could pass a town ordinance that what I say doesn't really matter.'

'That'd take the sting out of it, certainly. And if anything goes wrong, I'll say to them, "The fault lies not in your stars but yourselves." The phrase'll put some mysterious starry influence in the place of us, as the manipulating force. It's a classic two-choice limitation statement, neither option being the accurate one. Pure distraction, beautiful. D'you know what happened when Violaine was taken to court?'

'The judge told him, "Life isn't fair." '

'And Violaine pointed out that in the current context the judge was in a position to make it so.'

'A comment instantly stricken from the record.'

'Power's a funny thing.'

2

Meeow

*Government is like domestic abuse – it manages
to make the victim feel guilty*

The demon Rammstein, a serrated lord with a head like a
horseshoe, dragged a wooden crate through blasts of cold
electricity. Entering Sweeney's hangar-sized cavern, he stood
to attention in a black swallowtail coat.

The tyrannical mantis leaned its white glass head out of
the mist. 'Bit nippy, isn't it? Put on a radiator, there's a love.
This the crate? It'll need some refinement, but there we are.
The problem remains I eat souls, Rammy. How to get more of
them into my domain? How to make it attractive?'

'You could get someone to denounce it.'

'People don't pay much attention to that sort of thing these
days – if you weren't a preening cock-of-the-walk demon,
you'd know that. As Violaine said, "Any rate of resentment
lags behind the situation." '

'I am surprised to hear you quote your vanquished enemy,
Majesty.'

'Violaine's still here, Rammy. Hearing us, writing us down.
The fix is in, I'm sure of it. It hasn't been the same down here
since Dietrich hung up his spikes.'

'Dietrich – a vulturine demon, isn't he?'

'Paravamp. Draco class. He won't get much joy up there
with the 3Ds, I assure you. Too much prejudice. Body's no
place for a soul. And that lawyer, Max Gaffer.' Sweeney gave

a bark of laughter which darkened the sour yellow air. 'Crawled in here clutching hell by the hems, all missed beats and status anxiety. It made for a heavy satisfaction to have him fail like a mime in a blackout.'

'Where is he now, Majesty?'

'Off on some compensatory bender, I assume, with his tie in his pocket. I miscalculated sending old Rakeman above. Let's face it, he was just a bit of cold, bandaged stalk lightning. We need brute force, something that'll ignore whatever sorcery Juno throws at it.'

'You are still determined to destroy Barny Juno.'

'Of course. Revenge is more acceptable when completed than when left ragged and undone. Until it's finished people feel edgy. And old Violaine prophesied Juno was my nemesis. I think I'll send the demon Trubshaw to take care of him.'

Rammstein jerked a stare at his ratcheting Emperor. 'Isn't Trubshaw some kind of pack beast, merely?'

'Yes, a slob demon. Mud-encrusted dorsal studs in the old screw-in style. Forehead of Portland stone. That's the stuff. You Sawvillian fiends are good for the scary chat, but for unthinking action give me a dunce demon every time. The closest I got to Juno was by working two angles at once. Now I'm trying three – sending Trubshaw across, priming my inside man to act on his revenge premise, and something else.'

'Max Gaffer?'

'Gaffer's sawn through the brake cables of his luck. No. It's myself I refer to. The future will arrive when everyone has forgotten about it. What do you say to that, Rammstein?'

Rammstein bowed. 'Joyous blood flows through all the links in my chain, Majesty.'

Barny and the others were in the low-ceilinged cellar in which they grappled with the destitute oblivion of their employment. Some days the sorting office was a crust theatre of boredom and Edgy was free to elaborate on his latest cash cow as everyone else just sat there. 'So that's the plan, Bubba. I dress up in clown duds, stand around near some crates and get people to hand over everything of value. Oh, I might have to give them a soda or something, but basically, yeah, it's a lock.'

'It's screaming bloody death for everyone,' said B.B. Henrietta, and slammed a knife through a jiffy bag, pinning it to the sorting table.

'Well that's putting it a bit strong. Admittedly it won't work. What's the time?'

Barny shrugged. 'Five to eight, twenty to three . . .'

They stared a while at the Drop, an open corner into which they dumped most of the material which arrived here. It was basically a bottomless blank and wouldn't clog unless you threw too much in at once.

'I could dress myself up as a dog and threaten them. As Violaine said, "The human brain's a source of horror – there are reasons it's covered by a tarp."'

'Get some tips from Fang,' said Barny, 'he's a dog man.'

'He's a *bog* man,' Edgy told him, and gave a small gasp of exasperation. 'Barny, how many times do I need to explain about Fang being a zombie? He's one of the undead, Bubba, the *undead*!'

'I like him.'

'I love him, so what? Everything about him. Why are we here? I don't know what I'm saying any more!' And Edgy broke raggedly into coughing tears.

'Here he is,' Barny hailed as Fang wobbled down the steps.

The shambling cadaver wore boxing gloves for reasons he never discussed. He tilted toward the table and thudded down into a chair, a piece of his face shaking loose. 'My eyes have turned to mustard, lads.'

'Now that we're all here,' said B.B. Henrietta, 'except Gregor and Sags, and when Barny can stop looking at that stamped fly which looks like an asterisk, he has something to tell us which he claims is important.'

13

'I'm glad you asked,' Barny told her. 'Yes, as you all know, I live to care for the winged and stepping animals of the earth, and Karloff's stupid Circus is packed to the rafters with, Christ – beefy elephants, horses, marmosets, ostriches, belly dancers, rhinoceri, cats, and a snake called Magic Onion. It's Magic Onion I want to concentrate on first.' Barny told them about Mahru the Snake Charmer, who always became angry at the snake's slow emergence and picked up the bucket, hurling the viper into the audience with a roar. Barny had tried before to catch the beautiful creature and take it to safety, but there was never any telling which part of the crowd would be blessed with its sudden arrival. 'We have to position ourselves at points around the circle and be ready,' he told Edgy, Fang and B.B. Henrietta.

'Ready for a deadly snake to fly towards us,' said B.B. in a flat tone.

'And don't just sit there eating a ham sandwich or something,' Barny said vaguely.

'You subnormal,' B.B. shrieked. 'Karloff wouldn't think twice about lining us up on the ground and beckoning an elephant carefully forward.'

Barny disagreed, opening a colourful book about wild animals. 'This says, "Being large enough to live unchallenged, the elephant elects to do so at its own pace, while spurting people with water." God, I love animals.'

'Why?'

'Well, they don't ponce about. Except cats, of course. And they've got swivelling ears, so that makes up for everything.'

Edgy wiped his eyes. 'Everything, eh? Even lying around like a croissant? I don't think so.'

'Well I think it's a grand idea,' said Fang. 'And I for one will bake my own arse if it'll help.'

'It wouldn't really,' said Barny. 'But we need someone to work from the inside if I'm going to rescue any more lovely critters from the circus. Karloff wouldn't suspect if you returned to your brothers' trapeze act.'

14

Hunched under a low bare lightbulb, Fang was a sad figure of sinew and custard. He looked at his gloved hands where they rested on the table. For a while a rind of skin hanging from his forehead was the only part of him which moved. Then he said, 'Does anyone here mind if I—' and his head fell from his shoulders, banging loudly to the table like a rock.

Trubshaw stomped from a creepchannel exit, his heavy legs sloshing through gems and sleeping pills. He was basically a living spit-roast covered in armour plating. His mouth and neck were one and the same, his cranium ringed with ears like a crown. Raisin eyes surveyed the flaking car shells tilted in fields, the raggedy palm trees like exploded flags, the heat-white buildings in the distance. The whole day seemed exaggerated. He walked around the bleached and shattered bones of a Steinway spider and lumbered toward the town.

The carny was taking over the town square, acrobatic midgets pouncing across the rooftops to secure guy lines for the top canvas. These roustabouts shrieked constantly of 'the hell to come' and bit at each other, ululating strangely. The train had been cut up like a worm and Karloff's red and white striped wagon stood near the entrance to Yodel Erratum Street. He was making up at a lightbulb shrine spread with a chaos of fabulation powders, pinecones painted gold, funfair drugs, etheric ordnance and apples of black glass, when someone ducked in through the ladybug beads. 'One of the infernally modified,' said Karloff, finishing up, then turned in his chair and directed a chin like a gondola at Max Gaffer. 'And once a lawyer.'

'How do you know?'

'You lack the watermark of a soul.'

Gaffer tripped on a mash hammer as he advanced into the trailer, his sword-crowned head tangling with a sigil mobile. While in the service of Sweeney he had been placed in an editing bay and customised with a system of barbs and coldwater piping, leaving him with a body so absurd everyone was surprised he still felt able to put his name to it. He coughed in smuts of blusher. 'You've heard of Sweeney?'

Karloff avoided his eye. 'Some kind of overfed mosquito, isn't he?'

'Hardly. He's quite the king demon down there, oh yes – and I'm his right-hand man. I've made a lotta changes across there, put hell on the map, brought it up to date with modern marketing. And I could do the same thing for your operation.'

Karloff had taken up a clockwork violin and was leaning into it with a frown, a complex of agonies weaving through the air. 'This place has become hag-ridden with demons. Apparently two of them got married the other day and released a load of balloons.'

Gaffer was having to raise his voice. 'Too much for you to handle eh?'

'If you're really apprised of both situations, you'll know you demoted yourself when you went below.'

'Eh? Will you stop playing that thing?'

Karloff placed the instrument in its case and closed the lid, muffling the sound. He turned his grape-white face upon Gaffer. 'Bewilderment, the great leveller. Man lets himself be momentarily enchanted by what is strange and expensive, yet as beyond his control as all else in his life. Here in the Circus of the Heart's Shell we love sawdust because it's the telltale sign of a wasted afternoon.'

'So what's the attraction?'

'The spectacle with its lights and colours, the capering animals, the clowns plying their bloody trade, all this transports man from the mundane.'

'Mundane? If people want to see shrieking clowns they watch the Mayor give a speech. They want to see capering animals they go within a few yards of Barny Juno's house and in seconds their world is framed by the lion's jaws.'

'The lion – indeed. My lion, stolen from me by Juno. What's Juno doing these days?'

'Oh, that one,' said Gaffer, sitting down stiffly on a wooden chair. 'Claims his life has been bailed out by badgers. Kissed the snout of a hedgehog and smiled. Has eight hundred eels in his garden. Chose a point halfway through a funeral to abandon his trousers as a bad bet. Got a job as an exterminator and showed up at people's homes to polish the roaches and wash the gunk out of the flies' compound eyes.'

'So he's unrepentant.'

'I don't really know what that means. Something to do with curtain rails?' Gaffer picked up a framed poster printed in red, blue and brown ink. It portrayed confusion by the book, sprung from a carnival coffin – carrion clowns squabbling over the prey, elephants wearing stockings and suspenders, and Karloff himself with ears like shark fins, fanning razorblades like playing cards, his spiral hat towering and strange sprites capering in clouds about his shoulders. Gaffer squinted at one of these haunts. Was that a fanciful rendering of Skittermite whispering into Karloff's ear? Did the Fall Marshall have some connection with Sweeney? YOU WILL BE INJURED, the ad promised.

'I don't suppose you can box?' Karloff was saying. 'No? Shame – we've got a little fight set-up on the side. Well, apparently your life counts as much as theatre smoke. There's only one way I can think of that you could possibly help me. I need a gun. Should have brought my own, forgot about the paucity here. We were kicking through guns where we stopped last. When the scarship emerged into the square I heard the exit victim say something about a "Wesley Kern gun". What is that?'

'Part of our history,' Gaffer told him in a thoughtful tone. 'A man used the weapon to attack a bunch of people from the Tower. As it happens, I do know where you can find that item.'

'Brief Cheney when he returns from his chores, then we can discuss your employment.' He called after Max as the lawyer was leaving, 'Don't get in the way of the canvas crew!

Or the animals! And don't belittle them by saying "roar" or "chirp" – my animals are screaming in distress!'

Alone, Karloff looked out at a bunch of Cannon Church protesters shouting against the sacrilege of using a cannon in a secular strongman act. The window stained the people like wine, made them look like an ancient photograph. A thing is deemed sacred, he thought, when there's reason to keep us from dusting for fingerprints. Karloff picked up a copy of *The Blank Stare* which Cheney had dropped by earlier. The front page described the circus's arrival beneath the headline NO 'HORSE SENSE' WITH THESE BASTARDS and a photo of eleven clowns bidding to snog the same mare. Further down the page was a story about a man in trouble: 'Known to all as "Round One" and seemingly rambunctious, this fellow provoked a disturbance and smashed a restaurant window with his hips before shuddering at such speed the number of foamy flecks flying from his mouth surpassed an amount countable by this correspondent.'

'Round *One*?' Karloff mused.

Leapfrogging the burst sidewalks, a silver-painted midget with a set of useless wire wings and a head like a monkey-fist approached Del's Fright Foundry. The yard was filled with cans of lead, glass skulls and slot machines. 'Del?' Cheney called, entering the old garage to be confronted by a beetle like a giant black padlock rashed with rust.

Other massive sitch bugs filled the chamber, splayed legs snicking at every angle, and there in the corner of the nightmare was Del, satisfied, drinking a tinny. 'So you are back again, little man. I expected you when I went to the town centre for some paint and damned clowns were peering from every cranny. What's that stuff they're spreading on the front of the buildings?'

'Body fat,' said Cheney. 'Lard, to you.'

'Lard to me, eh? Is that so. And which of my things do you want this time?'

Cheney skirted the chubb beetle, patting its pelt of crumbled leather. The peeling gates of its wings flew open, startling him. 'Er . . . well, this hook masterpiece waving at me, for a start.' He looked around at the anthem statues and freaked exhibits which Del insisted on dragging through from another realm. 'You crave regular intimacy with a plane of bloody posts, Del, no reason why you shouldn't profit from it.'

'Just make your choice and leave.'

Here were anatomies like trash-and-wire sculptures, a sweating stone wrapped in rope, a totem pole with eyes of lye velvet and a heavy tar sentry. 'Well, I'll hire this little beauty, and mini-head here, this peppery shell, that one with drill-bit antennae, and that huge slab of stinking bacon. Not too venomous?'

'How much is too much?' Del grunted.

'Exactly. I'll send some clowns round to collect them. A few saddles and hawsers and we're laughing. Why struggle for horror when you can pay a small charge?'

That was the dodgem cars sorted. Cheney capered across town to the Church of Automata, slipping in through a window. The Grand Dollimo was standing on a platform above the slurry floor of the doll forge, reading a hinged mechanical book. Cheney walked along the scaffold toward him. 'You, sir – I have something to say.'

'What could possibly atone for your face?'

'Never mind all that. The Fall Marshall secured an arrangement with you when we were last in town.'

The Dollimo thumped the book closed, locking it. He regarded Cheney through a smoked glass mask. 'Work with him, do you? What do you do all day?'

'Mostly it has to do with frogs,' said Cheney diffidently.

'You study them?'

Cheney looked surprised. 'I avoid them.'

'You spend all day avoiding frogs?'

'Wouldn't you, if you could?'

'I am not in the business of mucking about. If this is all you learn, you won't have wasted your time.'

'Perhaps.'

'Not perhaps. My exalted frequency bars me from such horrors. Now, flesh into this room.' The Dollimo opened a bible door in the metal wall and ushered Cheney through. 'As Violaine said, "Research can be neither successful nor unsuccessful unless a particular conclusion is required." See how elegantly it works?'

In the dim vault two large Steinway spiders were crouched, black as old cola. One reared a little, showing a gob like a Pontiac grill.

'That's the one we call Sterling, the other is Dragbelly. They've been in here for three years, living on dustcakes and abducted children. Their articulation is rare but sudden.' The Dollimo noticed Cheney's deflated meekness before these hulking mechanisms. 'Not like the scalped piano in the museum, are they?'

'I . . . I don't think I know what you mean. I'm going now. I'll send some hoosiers to pick them up.'

'Tell Karloff to be careful. Give these the wrong pecking orders and you'll end up quiet in the grave, your brain turning to Marmite in your mouth.'

3

As Eels Go

*When someone starts saying 'vestibule', you
know you're in the wrong place*

Stealing down crystal streets of ground glitter, past tough
crocodilian trees and car metal too hot to touch, Karloff
neared the chaos of decks and gangways which was Barny's
house. Barny was standing outside, feeding a piglet with an
eye-dropper. 'Hello Karloff,' he called to the Fall Marshall.
'The sun rose this morning and light started ricocheting
around inside the marmalade.'

Karloff smiled winterly. 'I hate what I see – you live here?'

'Yes, ma'am.'

'I hear you've got hundreds of eels back there somewhere.
But why am I surprised by anything you do?' He spotted a
spaniel which nipped out through a catflap. 'A dog with
merry eyes and shaved legs, eh? Just look at the beast turn
its own left ear inside out. And to think that this is you at the
top of your game.'

Barny put the piglet down. 'Off you go, Mister Bond. Want
some lemonade, Karloff?'

'I'm afraid it's not that simple. What you pulled last time I
was in town. It wasn't polite. Fences, cages – they didn't last
long. Not with you putting ideas in those animals' heads.
You could almost mistake it for a plan. Species galore
becoming interested in freedom, brows creasing, the elephants talking about it openly. Bears looking at each other.

Biology darting forwards, doors torn from their hinges in a whoosh of escape, throats black with blood. A dozen blind-worms lost into the swamps. The pain and swelling was incredible. And then, the lion you stole, as pointless as a crop avenger. As Violaine said, "It's difficult to forgive someone for something if they still treasure their reasons for having done it."'

'Sling me that bit of gore will you?'

'Gore? Sling? Have you heard a bloody word I've said?'

At this point the lion skipped out through a busted gap in the house's wooden wall.

'So there he is,' nodded Karloff, 'raw in the universe.'

'Mister Braintree's one of my best friends. His one-inch claws are retractable and he has thirty teeth—'

'I know how many teeth he's got!' Karloff barked. 'Didn't I spend two years getting used to them before you stole the bastard?'

The lion had stopped, staring at Karloff with hard eyes. The Fall Marshall was about to sneer something like 'You've fallen arse backwards into flowers for the last time', when all at once he realised his danger, and froze. For some reason he noticed a bug tickling across the path like a living doll shoe. 'Well,' he said quietly. 'I intended to arrive and I did. A whisper means the same as a declaration.' And he backed very slowly out of his hazard.

As the zombie Fang approached the town square it became clear to him that Karloff would be using Grapefruit Integrity Swoon Street as the circus midway, filling it with stalls and sideshows. Between the circus wagons he walked into the odour of sawdust and all the cacophony of varicoloured idiots shouting the gibberish of their profession. He passed amid novelty morons and bollock-naked murderers, clowns throwing roses on to bonfires and Siamese twins joined at the eyelashes. The trick-riders spinning plate fungus seemed in his dead eyes to be freaky-assed and curious, throwing balls and rings into the air and catching them when they returned, only to throw them upward again as though nothing had been learnt by the previous experiment. He had been away a long time.

A pinhead in a jagged red suit hailed Fang from a half-built stall. 'Fang – still playing the decomposition card. You crawling back to your job?'

'That's right, Panatella,' said Fang, going over. He looked at the principles in pickle jars and shit-scary notices like WARNING: THE DEAD CUT THE LIVING'S STRINGS. 'My left shoulder is completely rotten. I'm pretty well patched up with gaffer tape, as you can see.'

Panatella sipped some acorn coffee. 'Well, you're dead and that's what's important. It's good to see you again.' He pulled something from the trash. 'Interested in this?'

'The shape is very puzzling, like a trumpet.'

'It's a trumpet, that's why.'

'No thanks, Boney, I better go find the troupe.'

Panatella pointed the way, his drumstick head swivelling to look.

As Fang walked on he was greeted by hoosiers, fire-drivers, some kind of human/chef hybrid, a sawback manticore and another creature which was half dogboy, half pot-roast. 'Why keep lustrous innards hidden?' asked old Shockheed Martin, whose transparent skin revealed his knotty plumbing. Everywhere wandered clowns tooled up with precision blades and bladders ripped out to dry before the pigs' dying eyes. A family of fire turkeys squabbled under a jacked-up truck.

'What are eyes?' came a woman's voice.

'Tears minus a wife,' Fang sniggered by rote, and went over to join the fortune-teller Sue Egypt, who sat on the chariot step of a black and red enamelled wagon.

'So here he is – Fang Palaton in pants so worn I can see my face in 'em.'

Fang laughed. 'Sue Egypt – she has attracted all the curses

of the Pharaohs and none of the mystery.' He sat down beside her. 'And as Violaine said, "Trousers are temporary, a bungled alliance."' They watched some seventh-circle clowns chase each other around. 'Just look at those mothers give each other a good kick in the pants. You can't beat originality. And who's that now?' He gestured to a passing hulk of muscle which had been topped with a head as an afterthought. The hairs on his arms were like spider's legs and he was covered in iron jewellery. But the expression on his face was mild.

'Dugway Thrax, the Beast Man. He's our latest strong guy, does the cannon act. He's double-hearted, doesn't like it here.'

'In Accomplice?'

'The circus, darling. Wants to settle down, become a townie. The way it is, he settles for five minutes, then gets shot into another postal district.'

'Another what? Well anyway, round here people only get shot out of a cannon when they're dead, that's what those priests are protesting about.' They watched the slow passing of a stilt monk with a business card for a mouth. 'So how's Karloff?'

She lit a small cigar. 'Oh, that one. He's almost come to believe his own tailor. Watch what he's got us about now.' She gestured to the rehearsing Floor Lobster Parade. Several were treadling by on miniature bikes. 'They've taught those nightmare vermin to do tricks.'

Fang gasped, his appalled face following the antics of a bug which turned to him with epoxy eyes. 'What else?' he asked her.

'You know the old pitbull spiders? He's using pianos now.'

'You don't mean—?'

'I mean it like it is, like it sounds. Steinway rumbles.' She plucked a rose out of thin air. 'You never know what's going to happen in the future, and when it does, it's best ignored. Locked in this rose is my one doubt. Time will release it.'

'He must know what he's doing. Horror wouldn't survive if it wasn't selling something somebody wanted.'

'Tell it to a tornado. Horror doesn't need to sell – it has power, does what it wants, takes what it wants, doesn't negotiate or ask permission. We don't buy a tornado – it drops down when it feels like it.'

'Okay, enough with the tornado. Where are my brothers? I'm as fit as a chimp, look at me.'

'You're a mess, honey.'

'So regret me.'

He followed her directions to a few practice bars set up in the dust yard. On the way he saw a sort of lard ghoul stomping north, its face the colour of dead chewing gum, its head crested with ear coral. Flesh bulged between its armour plating like wall insulation overflow. Accidents with accompaniment, thought Fang, that's us.

When he found his brother Squill, this tall tilt of sinew was hammering a hitching bar. His entire back was a furrow of green mud, but Fang recognised at once the glint of the wishbone at the nape of the neck. When the zombie sibling turned, he looked like he had inhaled his own face. The yellow jawbone worked. 'So, dirty eyes regard my efforts.'

'Hello, brother. Like all great men, I suffer the stigma of being timely.'

'You were never reckless enough for this troupe, Fangy. Or putrescent enough, even now. Are you using boot polish on that skin of yours?'

'I sleep in a tar pit.'

'There – ashamed to show your true lividity. Ladaat here lost both his eyes to decay years ago. His failures as a catcher have made our shows notorious since your departure. Eh, Ladaat?'

'I'm a catcher?' asked a bewildered corpse propped among some crates.

'Ladaat, my brother,' Fang hailed him. 'You have no arms.'

'And no way of telling,' laughed Ladaat toothlessly, his face covered in aphids.

'Good grief, he's not up to a show,' Fang whispered to Squill. 'He's no more than an inky post.'

'The people expect him – look at this review: "A thousand people died in the accident, which has been voted worst in the nation's memory." And your brother Enrico is still angry at your leaving. He will never allow you to rejoin. As the late great Bingo Violaine told it, "History is buried alive."'

'Ah, here he is,' came a voice, and Fang turned to confront a lurch of meat with a purple-black head massively swollen on one side. A dried eruption of brain matter tufted out like stuffing. 'Shiny as a cheat conker. In death as in life, eh?'

'He's been sitting in tar,' said brother Squill.

'Tar now is it?' rattled Enrico. 'And boxing gloves. Ashamed of your catching claws, eh? Didn't want to be reminded? Go to Karloff with your gloves, he's looking for fighters – you're not welcome among us.'

'Cut them off,' Fang instructed him.

Enrico looked sceptical, but reached for some shears. He snipped at the bindings, unwinding them and pulling the gloves off. They leaked embalming fluid. He cast them away into the dust.

'I didn't wear them for shame,' Fang told him, raising a set of leathery talons. 'But for preservation.'

Skirting around a cold troika sphinx from Del's collection deemed unfit for the dodgems, the demon Trubshaw passed a clown trailer on which the words

> *A clot of clowns will stop your heart*
> *And you will die just so.*
> *That's art.*

were unreadable by the monster dullard. His attention was transfixed by two scarlet valentine hearts which lay in the dust. Picking them up by the vein-strings, he peered inside the cavities. Heart gloves?

Four corpses assembled at the door to Karloff's candy-coloured wagon. The Fall Marshall scrutinised Fang through a pair of stained-glass spectacles. 'I know these other cadavers are viable – but you, Fangy? That duct tape around your neck? Your head's been off recently.'

'So?' piped up brother Enrico. 'That's what you want in a zombie, isn't it? A man so putrefied you could behead him as easy as a pint.'

'So whatever, I don't mind – if he can still do the job.'

'Nothing wasted there,' brother Squill chipped in. 'Hair over bone.'

'Get off your sky-high horse and give him another chance,' croaked Ladaat, staring through Karloff with empty sockets like large auxilliary nostrils.

Karloff gave something between a shrug and a nod. 'The path of circumstance runs infinite in all directions. We're a roomy canvas for death, lads – all of us.' And he gave a laugh hollow enough to shelter a fugitive.

4

To Here Knows When

Death is never at stake

The sky over the tent was unfocused. Barny and Gregor walked through the stench of sulphur and melon slices, punching away clowns and others acting goofy for cash, looking for the tall figure of Edgy in the bustling midway. They passed caramelised diplomats and frilled foetuses in limbo water. Kids were challenged to read a page in a leopard's cage, though none would successfully see the words, 'I have relieved you of minutes of the most powerless period of your life – the leopard could relieve you of more.' Here were blood-cough artists and lifelong eyeblink morsemen, their message ignored. Ince Elfshot was dealing out fish-head cards which disintegrated before they reached the table. Mr Macabre was displaying his insouciant control of a few daggers which he threw at and around a bikini-clad woman. Taken by surprise, she stood rigidly still in the act of buying an ice cream.

'Bits of my house are disappearing,' Barny complained to Gregor as they moved through the sideshows, chewing black wine gums with an aftertaste of turps. 'Whole lumps of the wall. I came back from staring at Chloe this morning and there were woolly monkeys all over the garden.'

'Well, I guess you know a thing's become a problem when the woolly monkeys start assembling.'

'Their vaulting-ladders have disappeared,' Barny explained. 'There was almost no way for them to spin upside down and engage in arse-display. Which is their main motive for waking up in the morning.'

'And mine. But I bet it only started happening since the circus came to town, right? I'll bet Karloff's behind it. How did the staring go, by the way? Chloe want you back yet?'

'Chloe wouldn't lie about something like that, and she's not crazy, so she must have meant it. I still need to see her, though. This time I had to submerge myself near the Juice Museum sea-doors and watch her when she came down to hang up some parchments for drying.'

'So you're spying on her, like a sick man.'

'With the help of some tubular bracken, yes. I nearly drowned. Heaven begins at her feet, Round One, I can't help it.'

'And they call me perverted, for having sex with my reflection in a shop window.'

'Yes,' said Barny, 'they do.'

Barny detected Edgy's voice above the neon-skeleton melodies of the calliope. The tuft-headed one was done up like some jester or spicy fool, baying rubbish at a medicine stall and apparently cashing in on the fad for cheaply made Aztec hope. 'And what in the name of boiling hell is this? you may ask. Temper, temper. From the land of bolted windows, air mothers and endless rain, I offer a connoisseur's grief. Agony Eight Hundred! Must you live? Do you think the womb is that personalised? Choose my teeth for your neck, ladies, I implore you! My merits warrant awe!'

'I don't understand what he's saying,' Barny murmured.

Gregor rushed up to Edgy's stall, aghast, and called back to Barny, 'I'll start interrupting him now.' Then he strained his face toward Edgy. 'What the hell d'you think you're doing, Edge? Take off those funny duds, the clowning union'll piss all over you. Agony Eight Hundred – what is it?'

Plantin Edge grinned wickedly. 'Don't worry, Round One. I stole some Cordial Perilous and mixed it down.'

'Cordial Perilous is half venom. It's a demon dare drink. What did you mix it with?'

'Venom.'

'Run for your life, Edgy.'

'Nonsense – I have to stick around to help with the snake abduction later on, don't I? But I'll enter the tent only when it's necessary. Clowns are in there by the million. They're killers, Round One. Running, bouncing, distributing deadly curses. By the time one of those bastards pops the wheels off his little car you might as well forget it.'

A jar of hazelworms clinked with wriggling.

'What if someone chokes on this stuff?'

'I'll address the complainer in barely audible tones, into his forehead, describing patiently my favourite furniture.'

'That's your answer to everything,' said Gregor, and walked back through the crowd to Barny. 'He'll wait for the signal.'

A silver-painted midget was yelling as they approached the giant tent flap at the end of the street, 'Step right up if you consider it's any of your business. Entry is simplicity itself – step and step and step this way, and be prepared for feats of strength and agility which will explode your eyes! Our clowns are donning their battle pants even now, think of it! Trials of mesmerism, conjuring, legerdemain and related larking about. By God, we'll test your patience! And no respite from boisterous diabolo jugglers whose expressions make clear to one and all that they are savages at heart! You want disaster? We think of little else! You want silverfish? Dozens pulse up the walls! I remember a lad all happy and aglow when he entered – his head exists on top of a staff now, unable to beat off the flies! That's right, in you go, my lovelies! Yellow moments remain unsubverted – for ever!'

Barny and Gregor passed near the vinyl smile of Cheney, then the flap had slapped closed behind them.

They had stepped into a chaos of swooping spotlights. The entire round of the town square had been roofed with a canopy, turning the centre of town into one giant big top. Grandstand seats were built against the surrounding buildings, the balcony of Rudloe Manor forming a royal box. Rudloe's face hung gormless in its frame.

The square was rammed. Barny didn't feel like he was in Accomplice town as he and Gregor found their seats and cold blue air flashed around them. Whips, capes and parasols hung from the statue of Bingo Violaine, making it a prop rack for the Fall Marshall. Kerosene was burning in raised pan lamps. Concession barkers saddened kids in the audience by throwing gold ingots disguised as candy bars, cracking them upside the head, and then the disappointment. Through the swerving searchlights and blaring horns, Barny spotted B.B. Henrietta on the opposite side, fast asleep, and across the way sat Sags Dumbar, whose aqueous bag of a head could mean only failure. 'Keep your eyes peeled for Magic Onion,' Barny hushed aside to Gregor.

The square became deaf and blind.

A sparkling infection of green metallic curtain bloomed with a spotlight, then parted. A banana-moon face leered under a tall humbug hat. 'Here I am, first poisoned and last dead! Just as God, under the most costly of canopies, rigs agonies for its dulled curiosity, we operate in infamy, trading in transgressions beyond number, accidents beyond definition, and all the awfuls of nightmare. We stoop to intervene in your drab affairs! I'm sorry to say some of you will be destroyed, for that is part of delivering more than mere pleasure and fancy! Come among you via the chill wonders of the Trans-Reptilian Express . . . The Circus of the Heart's Shell, one immense indiscretion!'

An explosion went off and a storm of waivers fluttered down on the audience.

Karloff now hung off Violaine's statue at a jaunty angle, gesturing about the ring with a red cane of spine diamond.

31

'Big-name attractions crash to earth! Quick nannies sharpen their knives! See our clowns, empty flesh fetches who simply won't keep their private hell to themselves!'

The calliope struck up a reverse dirge as a colour flurry of clowns with crayola claws spread on to the hippodrome track, spinning paraphernalia gemmed and striped, their opaque eyes revealing nothing. Tumbling in attack jackets and zigzag pantaloons coordinated to some polychrome hierarchy of recent invention, they enraged all by throwing walnuts into the audience.

'Daring us to smash their porcelain heads – but could we bear to touch? And if silence wore a beard, its name would be Mr Macabre. His magic is so modest in astonishment it must compensate in disgrace. Yes, a shiny foreigner is standing without shame, conjuring brains from your bonces – which surely were not there when he reached out his hand? His last performance ended in a chaos of industrial glass, shattered sawblades and gashed volunteers! Observe!'

A fragile girl in dragonfly coveralls assisted as Mr Macabre, a square yellow man with eyes like joy-buzzers, rolled a black box into the ring. A sheet-blade projected above it. It was made up to look like an old cabinet radio, a coffin for electricity, the blade its aerial. 'There are many ways to irritate,' the magician shouted. 'Whistle "thank you" instead of saying it. When asked for directions, point the way with your tongue. And best of all, bisection with a saw, oh yes. Quickly you applaud, though clueless. You disgust me.' He climbed into the box, lying back and closing the two half-lids. 'Would someone of such skill as I spend time constructing an object without purpose? An old radio made of skin, it makes a sound like storms. Its inner workings are jet black, packed so dense with ants their blackness has given up and turned inside like a migraine. And don't your desperate eyes quicken and become riveted as I tell you that to prove the blade is real, I'll test it on my own body rather than standing within reach of the trapdoor release button. Oh God—'

The girl was drizzled with blood as the blade shunted down. Clowns capered over, running the box out of sight as Karloff watched.

'Damn it all, he deserved better. A lot better. And here, because I take an interest in you for which you should be grateful – Gemini Dog! By-blow of the frenzied union of a realtor and a human being. If his face offends you, all complaints here, in the fire. Fire is born old, ladies and gentlemen. Whisper it.' A piece of folded meat wobbled across the flashing plain on a tripwire tricycle lethal to anyone as Karloff raved on and the ring increased in resolution. Macabre's shaken assistant was being taunted and attacked. 'The Killer Midgets! There's a bounty on their heads! Staggering Joe Almighty – there's more to his antics than meets the eye! Kevin, he of the Smashed Face and Drinking Habit! Ten Beans Stapled to a Stupid Sod, ladies and gentlemen! My mother, everyone! And here is Kaspar Blenny, a man made entirely of ear tissue!' A bloke bent over in a bow, and flipped quickly up again. 'Now you will see a creature as rare as a fish with shoulders, ladies and gentlemen – a fish with shoulders!' A fish with shoulders was wheeled on in a pram. 'Even the most learned conversation yields to a warning of fire – and the Trauma Clown imbibes to be ablaze and a lesson to us all! Winner of the Clown d'Or, it's like he's in the room!'

A death-headed harlequin stalked into view, antics galore about him, and an oiled hoop was set alight.

'The burning hoop, ladies and gentlemen, symbol of life – one big flaming zero! How long will it take for the maestro to eat it? Yet in this way he will challenge the world!'

The etiolated jester neared the hoop, his white face glistening like a soft-boiled egg. His entire head had been dipped in greasepaint. As he flipped his mouth open and brought it to the flames, fire flashed across and ignited his cosmetic skull. He was a shrieking scarecrow, standing in place like a thing planted, the Killer Midgets dancing around him.

'So many questions, so little time! Longer backs are all the rage, baby. Observe as Bibi Mahru Blitz deploys the biggest armoury of charms since the serpent prompted Eve! The viper Magic Onion resides in that urn – watch Bibi Mahru's efforts!'

The audience were by now weeping with disappointment. As Mahru sat cross-legged before the urn and began parping on some sort of bugle, Barny leaned over to Gregor. 'There he is – get ready.' Gregor lit the end of an arrow and fired it into the tent wall near the entrance.

'The Beast Man – rubbish, albeit I have tremendous respect for his physical strength! See him climb into the cannon and leave it at a blur! No homoerotic vision has been so bluntly metaphorical since the days of Sparta! Beware, the Beast Man!'

The grim and muscular Dugway Thrax flexed his arms redundantly and then clambered into a cannon which was immediately fired off by a few clowns. There was a hell of a lot of smoke, out of which his body flew and zoomed through the balcony window of the Mayoral Palace, the Mayor himself flinching like a failure. Cannonites roared their disapproval, waving banners which stated, ELAPSED GHOULS SHOULD CLEAR THE WAY.

A rhino was lumbered across the showground. 'The Indian army would train rhinos to ride at the head of battle,' shouted Karloff, 'scattering the enemy! But for our purposes, the Fatal Rhino merely trots like a mule, an insult to his heritage! And look there – a pig with a nose like a punctured tankard!'

A pig skittered in, disappearing into the chaos somewhere. 'And no good can come of these aerial cadavers. Look above, in bird-light heights – the Flying Dead Brothers! Limbs busted aside, skin shredded like rind, spraying blood and gutwater where they go, they really are brothers, ladies and gentlemen!'

High in the rigging, Fang and his brothers began the gymnastics of entropy. These reaching armatures of tendon and catgut screamed quite audibly that 'This'll never work' as they flailed past the tarp lights. Coffin dust sprinkled the audience.

'There on the hanging rings it's quite dicey! Eternally famished, they gnash at the air, gnash at the air, gnash at the terrible air! And above all, see our new addition, a freak of purity, a bandaged lamb, captive in a barcode!' The spotlights converged upon a large cage which hung from the distant ceiling. It contained a winged angel, glowing white as though over-exposed. 'The Caged Angel, Evangelica of Rust, Eden Vulture in its own light. It's the oldest story in the world!'

'That's Mike Abblatia,' said Gregor, squinting up, 'the car salesman. I'd always thought he was more sensible.'

Squill and Ladaat collided in midair, smashing like kites. Pieces of them fell, spinning around a central tangled mass. 'Acrobats often tire of audacity and catch the idea of landing in the stalls, bless 'em,' laughed Karloff as the twisted gristle hit the crowd.

Alerted by the spreading conflagration near the entrance, Edgy ran into the big top to do his part in the snake rescue just as Mahru lost his patience. After resorting to the shout of 'Emerge, emerge!' and repeated shaking of the tub, the snake-charmer finally took it up and with a cry of 'I *said* you'd show yourself, Magic Onion, and—!', swung the container, ejecting the snake into the air. Edgy took it right in the eye and fell in the path of circling animals and bounding clowns. He lay amid the danger like a used firework, elephant legs stamping past him.

'Edgy, stop saving your energies and grab the beautiful serpent!' Barny yelled, turning aside to find that Gregor had disappeared. The crowd were panicking due to the quickly spreading fire and Barny shoved through people and smoke toward the ring, where Edgy seemed to be groggily awakening.

'That boil-in-the-bag fakir has lost all self-control,' Karloff proclaimed. 'And what's this? The lads are surprising me with new business! A clown in the melancholy vagabond style. Tolerate his ancient buffoonery if you can! See the other clowns chase him as he tries to steal Magic Onion! Check out the hairstyle like an exploded cheroot. To the extent that he waves his arms at us all he seems friendly and energetic. As Violaine said, "A good leg will know when to kick, know when to run, and handle the transition quickly." '

Bent sparks quicked past Edgy's screams as he rampaged away from the clowns, holding the viper Magic Onion away from himself. Behind him a new spurt of clowns roared into frenzy, baying through acrylic faces. Spotting Barny, he threw the snake to him just as a clown with a kitchen haircut and carnation barred his way. The clown's face darkened like a lightbulb when Edgy ploughed him to the ground, sand spraying like pepper.

Above the scene, blood hanging out of him, Fang swung at ease on the showboat bar. The top of his head had been exploded into tatters, which flapped glamorously as he waved to the swarming crowd.

'Join us again for our full performance,' Karloff proclaimed as blown sparks flurried around him. 'Watch when it profits you, ignore when it profits you, deplore when it profits you, war when it profits you.'

Barny ran into the flames.

Gregor wandered through the sideshows, ignoring the potato hospital and the Staring Cannibal booth. He had long ago visited a 'Trouble Me Not' tent full of witheringly sarcastic mirrors which corrected people's grammar and told them to stop giggling like tarts. That garish enterprise, set up in the pennygrounds by Prancer Diego for no apparent reason, was destroyed by a posse of fire-wielding townsfolk. The chaos of burning mirrors had called ironic abuse to the onlookers as the glass warped and burst in, impressing no one.

But Gregor had never visited a real hall of mirrors, and now he found one. The steps had surfaces red as a heart and an arched sign over the entrance said, DOUBTS TANGLE INSIDE A STACK OF DOORS. SHALL YOU ENTER? The door handle was a shock, apparently made of nuts. Strange devices infected the architecture in the entrance hall and a tailor's dummy, symbol of hellish intoxication, hung suspended from the encrusted blue sky of the domed ceiling. Striped walls messed with Gregor's perspective. For a quick-assembly gig it was impressive.

He advanced into the dark mirror hall, eyes readjusting as his own chubby image stepped into view. He had to admit it, he was a lovely sight. Rather than being simply reflected, his image seemed to disturb some sort of molecularity on the surface, which swirled into place after his movements. The very darkness swirled with brownian particles. This mirror flowed into the next, decanting him like wine. The frames were bottle-green and each was crested with a stupid slogan:

Can't sleep? Stick head in mill.

Lack imagination? Why not be a lackey?

Gore in the attic? Keep embroidering.

He looked at the hall as a whole. In each glass his own face spectated, a row of vacancies. He moved and looked, his limbs stopping in the distance. He shook his head and it dribbled along the wall like a stain. He was everywhere, a god in invincible trousers. The lights started frazzling, spatting on and off and burning the air. He was too much for them, even in the midst of this cheap, sinister hoax. His image bulged through everything, intrinsic as love.

Laughter burst from his face and was instantly blocked off as a cold hand discovered his mouth. 'Poison can appear precious,' said the voice of Karloff Velocet close by his ear. 'Maggots tickle the ears of the dead. The only puzzle worth doing is one which notices when it's solved – something is activated.'

Gregor's senses exploded in an opulent apocalypse and he stormed into darkness.

*

In fact Karloff had heard a bit of a commotion while passing the Hall of Mirrors and popped in to check it out. There he found a ridiculous gutbucket smashing seven shades of glass out of the mirrors by rushing upon them with his groin. By the time Karloff had recovered from walking in on this wall-to-wall incompetence, the strange fellow was having a convulsive fit on the floor, folded up like a discarded clay figure. Karloff did not in fact mutter in Gregor's ear and he didn't say anything clever or enigmatic. But he did recognise this as the man in the news report, the roaring boy known as – what was it? – 'Round One' or 'First Round'? Here was someone he could use.

5

The Big Huge

Always pick up a fish by the ears

His boots munching across the sand, E.H. Hunt carried a load of wood past a dissolved causeway to his construction area beside the gulping sea. He dumped it next to the hammered frame of spars and, gasping, addressed the Announcement Horse. 'This beard of mine conceals the fact that my chin was eaten off by a giant bass. Years ago.'

No one had ever pronounced with certainty upon the Announcement Horse's species. It seemed unacceptable that it was simply a heavy iron horse which made an occasional declaration and never moved a muscle. 'What did I tell you,' boomed the sepulchral steed, 'about your chin and beard's equal unimportance.'

Hunt sat on the wooden travelling chest he took with him everywhere. 'I had trouble interpreting the notes of your speech so I concentrated on the words, which were all about death and strength and gate posts pushed two ways at once by a titan – the bloody fool need only push gently and hey presto, ah we're none of us perfect.'

'I stated that "Infinity has so much structure, it has no structure". Thus evil's limbs may believe themselves the heart. There is no heart.'

'I knew a fella,' said Hunt, 'who carved gargoyles out of pear wood so that with the rain and all they got smoother and younger as the years passed. Finally they were like babies. Well, I liked the idea so I carved a figurehead like an old woman. What with the surf and spume she got younger and younger, a beautiful babe, then more like an actual baby, then a smooth skull, and finally a sort of doorknob. Ah, I should have thought it through. The Skipper stabbed me in the abs for that little bit of mischief.' Hunt glanced at his sleeve capstan and said, 'The show'll be winding down. Maybe that's enough timber for the hull.'

Barny and the bag-headed Sags Dumbar carried Edgy between them like a piece of frayed rope. 'Fang should eat more,' Barny said. 'He's skin and bone.'

'He's meant to be,' Edgy moaned. 'He's a zombie.'

As Ladderland came into view, Barny saw that the ground floor wall was missing. He thought at first that it must have been Karloff's doing but the lion loped on to the porch, untroubled.

They dumped Edgy on a sofa. 'I can't feel my arse,' he moaned.

'Well that's no great loss,' said Barny, and took Magic Onion from around his neck. 'Where's my house disappearing to?'

'I'll have the roast beef platter,' said Sags Dumbar.

Barny wandered across town to the canyon where doomed Eddie Gallo was said to be rebuilding the flyover. Sure enough, there were planks galore piled ready. Surprised at doomed Eddie Gallo's gall, Barny set about taking the wood back before Gallo should return. As Violaine said, 'The holder of stolen goods must have the patience and serenity of an oak.'

Dozens of punters surrounded an earth clearing in a small side tent. Karloff pushed Gregor through the crowd. 'Watch closely, First Round. Our roasted champion the Trauma Clown is facing a new challenger there, the one with the crown of ears. He showed up with some old found gloves and a clueless expression.'

Gregor stared at the mayhem on the dirt-floor boxing ring – a sort of living practice bull was taking the Trauma Clown apart with ease. Flents of skin flew off as though from a circular saw.

'Full of belligerence and moxie, that one, eh Fall Marshall?' commented the midget Cheney.

'If that fella punches your face, your head snaps back,' Karloff agreed. 'He's going postal.'

'Going what?' asked Gregor.

'He'll smash your pegs down your throat.'

The Trauma Clown shattered as though its skull was fragile as a poppadom. Cheney was already in there, sweeping away blank laminated puzzle pieces as a knocked lightbulb swung to illuminate and darken a red scrawl on the canvas wall: DROWN THE KNIGHT AND ARMOUR IS UNLOCKED BY WATER AND WORMS.

'I'm reluctant to characterise it as a fight at all,' remarked Karloff. 'It was more like a sort of decision against the other fellow's existence. Did you get a name from this roly-poly monster, Cheney?'

'Calls himself Trubshaw.'

'Then so shall we. Prepare yourself, First Round. In two days you will fight our new champ to a standstill.'

'I don't know how to fight this thing,' Gregor whined. 'What's wrong with its legs? It's probably some sort of demon or a thing grown from evil dough. It's wearing armour. D'you expect me to just dance around wearing two giant cherries on the end of my arms until I die?'

'You'll see no signs saying not. Put him through his paces, Cheney.'

As Karloff left the game tent and crossed the circus back yard, he saw Barny passing by with a few planks. 'Barny Juno!' he hailed him.

Barny looked over. 'Yes, ma'am?'

Karloff gasped in exasperation but reset his features. 'Come here, Nature Boy, we've business to discuss.'

Barny wandered after Karloff toward his trailer. As Barny passed, a barrel monkey in a velvet jacket and cap immediately tore off its clothes and followed him. Barny leant the planks against Karloff's wagon and stepped up into the gemlike gloom. Karloff was brewing chain tea and sorting a few bugs. 'How did you enjoy the show?'

'By setting myself a distracting task,' said Barny. He was looking at a poster portraying carnival pathologies in reverse colours. In small type at the foot of the turmoil were the words, 'No attraction dies nameless.' Chittering, the organ chimp jumped on to his shoulder.

'Your open face blasphemes the struggles of man,' Karloff observed.

'Why isn't the Caged Angel on this poster?'

'That flying flesh crucifix is a very recent addition.'

'He's a grease monkey from Spacey's Gas Station.'

'Perhaps he *was*. We acquire curiosities where we go. Freaks and novelties. The chefs are missing their horrific cupboard lord and we have a new exhibit – The Famine Siren, a mermaid of bones. Why, I've a little item here you may recognise.' Karloff brought a lobster trap from beneath his makeup table – it contained a dog-sized bug with many pale legs. 'Here in the wicker cage, this came from your friend Sags's head, yes? It's a Varney bug. Your friend had a bad idea, the worst. When involuntary truths volley from the face they can do a lot of damage on the way out.'

'You've been in the sorting office.'

'Cheney has – he's paying several visits about town. This is a fertile recruiting ground for abductees. But perhaps we can come to an arrangement. You return the lion, the snake you just stole and certain other animals by way of compound interest and I return your angelic friend to you. The perfect sacrifice meets the perfect fool.'

'And I suppose you don't want me to tell anyone that the

fab new zombie you announced is just an old one which had quit and returned.'

'A trifle.'

'I won't be bought that easily!' Barny shouted, kicking the trap aside and standing. 'And as for giving you any animals . . .' And he held the poster in front of his face, pushing his whole head through the tearing paper and screaming in a surprising way, his tongue extended.

When Barny was gone, Karloff wandered over to Rudloe Manor to chat to the Mayor.

The Mayor was sitting there like a paperweight and talking on the phone as the huge armoured bat Dietrich Hammerwire perched on a sideboard, gnawing through the shelled back of a floor lobster.

'Ah, the left and its right hand,' said Karloff, 'the right and its left.'

'Crunches the undersecretary under slowly lowering ceiling, you say? I don't know, Verbal – sounds expensive. I'll have to call back, I have a visitor. Goodbye.' Mayor Rudloe replaced the receiver and turned his attention to Karloff as the Fall Marshall sat opposite. 'Karloff. When I offered space to your shortcomings it wasn't my understanding that you'd plunge the square into darkness and fill it with bone-shivering mutants. Our municipal fittings have become silted up with dead clownflesh and cancer confetti.'

'Your mouth's off-kilter, Mayor – have you recently suffered catastrophic chin failure, by any chance? And why have you got a picture of brutal damnation hanging behind you?'

'The world's come to a pretty pass when a ringmaster can't tell the difference between a portrait of me and a picture of brutal damnation.'

'You might consider that for a campaign slogan.'

'I believe doomed Eddie Gallo is already using it. Have a look at this. I've underlined the relevant passages.'

'None of it's underlined.'

'None of it's relevant. Drop it in the bin there. That document was doomed Eddie Gallo's latest manifesto, *Will I Ever Learn*? The clueless muppet proposed some sort of scheme for growing corn on the cob in his eyesockets. His timid and compromised antics will ram him head first into hell.'

'Nothing to worry about then, eh?'

'Isn't there. Have you noticed the cornice damage from that meat-head you fired in here? And I've been looking at this skit you gave me to memorise. It's bloody death and bursting stomach walls for everyone. Do I really have to swap jokes and drolleries with you in the full gape of public scrutiny?'

'It must be seen and heard if it's to work as entertainment. It's similar to the shrillness principle. Even Violaine said: "For propaganda to resist erosion, calm voices must be seen as more absurd than hysterical ones." What's the problem?'

'Well, this sort of thing. "I say, I say, I say, what do you get if you cross a barber with a camel?" "I don't know, what do you get if you cross a barber with a camel?" "An abomination." I mean, it's appalling. And this bit where I "pull out a fireman's hose and take ten years off the audience's life". The list goes on. The safety culture of endless curtailment depends on respect for my authority, especially with the blood levy coming up.'

'Pardon, Mayor,' the demon Dietrich chipped in, 'but the image is one of folksy participation. All in it together. A leech only works up close, after all.'

'Your hood ornament's right, Mayor – public opinion's an unending race for mutual peer approval. That and fear's why they bleed once a year. We've all heard about the levy skeletons buried behind the shed.' Karloff jerked a thumb in the direction of the blood clock. 'That bit of gruesome chronometry justifies nothing, as you know.'

Rudloe uttered a wordless grumble. 'In the final analysis I serve an implacable mass of lard with an insatiable lust for blood. Unfortunate, but there we are. When you're in a position where you must make unpopular, indeed disastrous, decisions every day, before you know it you've got chops like these . . .' He pulled his cheeks out like empty pockets, then released them, giving up.

'You could escape.'

'Outside, you mean, through that icy razorbahn? I've heard enough about the world out there to know I've a good thing.'

'That's not quite what I meant. Have you considered soul secretion?'

'I've heard of the practice. Certain lawyers have attempted it.'

'My own assistant Cheney put his into the head of a sweetpea, a particularly short-lived flower.'

'An annual.'

'Indeed. When it rotted down, Cheney's soul was released and probably resides in several worm families today.'

'Now, now,' Rudloe chided. 'There are worse places to reside than in worm families.'

'If you say so, old boy,' frowned Karloff. 'Now, it's not generally known that every one of my clowns is soulless. They're a handful of functions, merely – where their makeup ends their bones begin. The souls are stored in a cold grey stone buried deep in a fallow field. It's my belief that Bingo Violaine did something similar.' He produced a rusty star-shaped box from beneath his jacket. 'I can offer you this in return for a simple service.'

'That's a Steeping Template,' said the demon Dietrich with sudden curiosity. 'Or cannari cage. Avatar-made for soul storage.'

'A handy bolt-hole for the day your enemies come for you,' Karloff continued, nodding. 'Or put half in there and the rest reels in at death.'

'Dietrich, leave us,' said Rudloe, with a flick of his hand. Dietrich bowed his claw-hammer head and stepped out. 'What do I do in return?'

'I've proposed a trade of talent with Barny Juno.'

'That subnormal? He once came in here and threw a rock-hard cooking apple into my eyes.'

'He's to hand over his beasts and I'll hand over an angel which I've discovered to be of rather callow vintage.'

'He's agreed to this?'

'He led me to understand he needed twelve hours to decide. But he'll do it, I'm sure. When the magical exchange takes place at the end of our final performance, I require it to be witnessed by representatives of each facet of this community – you, Mayor, and doomed Eddie Gallo, Dietrich, a few industrialists like King Verbal, Beltane Carom the ordered arcane, the Grand Dollimo, Del and Prancer Diego, the stupid bastard who mucks about. All must witness that the lion has been returned voluntarily.'

'The shaman too? Oak law and hedge saints, that's all I need. Why do you have to make a spectacle out of everything?'

'I've got detail all over my face,' said Karloff. 'I can do anything I like.'

The Mayor's face cleared like he was feeling strange and weightless. He shook his senses. 'That's the most marginal definition of freedom I've ever heard.'

'Freedom must needs be marginal and so my particularly marginal definition of it affected you unusually—'

'Oh, shut up. What are you doing now?'

'Pissing off the balcony,' Karloff called back. 'I suppose I might see my way to going on the rampage later, if I find a window.'

'Your circus is a contaminant, Karloff,' shouted the Mayor.

'We are chaos.'

'So are we – but yours is different from ours.'

Chloe sat in the bone room with her father, an old man with a soul as real as a cat's torn ear. 'I told him he should be more giving, think more about what other people need.'

Gully sipped tea from a tarot cup. 'And what did he say?'

'Something about feasting harmlessly and hot upon me like a lion. A lion won't stop at looking, he said.'

Gully Low gave a tired smile, his face as grey as a dead feather. 'He dotes on you like a sucker dart.'

'If he understood people as well as he understands animals . . .'

'He'd give them all room in that decked hill station of his. I remember the days it began to get hot around here. It changed everything. Instead of being broken up in sharpness and rain, the land became heated like one large room. Tropicalia was a fashion for a while, then people had to deal with it for real. The chill was an old excuse for separation. And so a thousand new excuses were found. I get the feeling Juno doesn't have that fear – he's just a little distracted.'

'Did you hear the seadoors just now?' Chloe frowned. She stalked carefully out of the little room and peered through her lopsided hair at the sloping rock corridors of the Juice Museum.

'This sign looks pretty easy to read,' came a voice. 'Let's take a look at it.'

Chloe ducked back into the bone room. 'Father, someone's broken in!' But Gully Low was drowsing, a headache flower blooming in silence at his shoulder. His tea genie began seeping into view, fringed in shrivelling air.

She returned to the corridors, searching through silence. Mackaw wood, Sahara bibles, the Cyril Manifesto, D.G. Croley, boxes of crystal teeth. Everything seemed forgotten in place.

But down in the grotto, on the narrow ledge toward the low cave mouth, cotton candy shreds blew, caught in the fence wire.

6

Helterpolitik

When all history's lessons have been given, it begins to cycle

Barny entered the lambent green of the walled garden. The shaman sat at the centre of involutes of truth, consulting a nerve almanac.

'I need your advice, Beltane Carom. Something practical, though. That Power Shout you taught me was the crappiest thing I ever did.'

'Once again you interrupt my meditation with trifles.'

'How did you know about that? I refused it.' Barny sat down on the hot patterned flagstones. 'The deal was, I return the lion and he returns the angel.'

'How did you leave it?'

'I led him to understand I needed twelve hours to decide.'

'Pushed your head through a poster, eh? Well, I'm sure your lion could find his way home. And if not, you could always follow Karloff's scarship into the creepchannel, with a suitably shielded car. Mike Abblatia could fit one up after you've sprung him, perhaps.'

'But why does the ringmaster hate me so much? One lion I stole, and before that a camel, old Mister Bailey. And this time a snake. But why all the bile?'

'Probably it's demon-spun.'

'That's what you always say.'

'Truth isn't a bee, Juno – it doesn't die after it's stung you.

Even you can't have failed to notice you attract hellfire like an intake fan.'

'These demons, where do they live?'

'In the brief darkness hidden in the middle of summer.'

'That's where they hide?'

'They don't need to hide. Neither does good need to hide. Wholeness is not purity. Wholeness is life, the lot.'

'I don't get it.'

Carom thought about it. 'Put it this way. That colossal demon, Sweeney, the acid one who dislikes you. It nestles there in ashspace thinking it's king shit. But it's not the source of anything.'

'I still don't understand.'

'Well. An octopus has many arms, yes? And every bit of every arm is octopus, every inch. It's not bird or dog, right? Evil's the same. There's no real king or centre to it.'

'What's an octopus?'

Carom had kitchen scales, the bowls of which were concave mirrors – these could weigh the despair of any face reflected there. He peered into this now and the bowl crashed to earth. But it seemed it was freighted with more than mere exasperation at his guest's stupidity. Carom looked up as Barny stood to leave. 'Juno. Insanity happens when all your adjustments to the world meet up by accident. You don't have any adjustments. I hope you never do.'

Barny left the garden and was about to head off to Karloff when the stringy Plantin Edge lurched up with his arse in a sling.

'Hello Edgy – has your arse healed enough to give you any pleasure?'

'There's more to pleasure than a healthy arse, my friend.'

'Where's Gregor?'

'Shaped like a pear.'

'Where, I asked.'

'Oh – well, sleeping with his lack of money, probably. Or

trying to sell the new line of Condemnation Cards they've got at Stampede.'

'That stall of yours was rubbish, by the way.'

'I suppose it didn't help that I advertised the fruit as "Treetop bounty, dispossessed and huddling in our bowl". I'm going to open a chain of dry cleaners called "Ruination" instead. Yeah, we're all in it together, that's the idea. You been consulting the guru?'

'Karloff's proposed a trade – the Abblatia angel for my lion. I was asking the shaman for advice.'

'No need, Bubba. I've just been chatting to a fella with bacon hair over at the midway. Tipped me off on a dirtfight in a side tent in the circus yard. Called the Tar Baby Concerns. There's a fighter called the Masked Inconvenience who was in absolute cracking form at the trials apparently. Got YOUR FACE HERE tattooed on his fists. That's the kind of brutal moron we need.'

'I haven't got the readies.'

'Listen to me Bubba, it's a sure thing. You bet on him and winner takes all – propose that to Karloff. He's not a gum-shield with gossamer wings like some of the fellas I've recommended in the past.'

'You're dreaming.'

'You are super-wrong, my friend. Each finger as heavy as a marble egg, that's the form. The Masked Inconvenience – there's power in mystery. It's a lock.'

Barny thought about it. 'I suppose it could save a lotta trouble. You know more about this stuff than me.'

'Great,' said Edgy, walking on, and called back over his shoulder, 'Apparently he's up against some amateur called Trubshaw.'

As Barny continued toward the town centre, listening with a smile to some low-key barking off a distant dog, he nearly collided with Chloe Low, her face milk-pale, her eyes like liquorice, her cherub gob working like a hypnotist's spiral. 'Barny,' she breathed. 'I think someone stole the Wesley Kern gun – it's all that's missing. Remember the story I told you? Kern made the gun in a dental forge with boneseed and headwater. Then he went up the Tower of Nowt and shot at the Mayoral Palace. They made it seem afterward that he'd fired on innocents.'

He remembered – Kern had tried a sort of shooting and screaming gambit before Barny or Chloe were born.

But Barny could only stare up and down her as though at a golden ladder. The heaven he lived in her minutes felt like contraband now.

She nodded forlornly. 'I sense something. Tragedy's at hand.'

'I love you.'

'This isn't about you, Barny.'

'I know.'

'Or your animals. People first, Barny. It's your civic duty.'

Without understanding why, Barny felt disappointed in her. He put the feeling away.

'I have to get back to the Juice. Beware the clowns.' She walked away. Barny watched a rust-coloured insect land on the white landscape of his hand.

The daredevil Beast Man, Dugway Thrax, dared to dream of an edible meal, but despite the new boxer Gregor's warnings he visited the Ultimatum Restaurant and dragged the challenger with him. Intent over the table they kept an eye on the menu, a translation of which they listened to in a spirit of horror and fright. 'What's deathhead chowder?' Thrax asked the waiter.

'Gulch bulbs in blue ink, throats leaking old rain, disarmingly poisonous eye-roots and a tangle of stinking weeds. With French fries.'

'Well, fries at least. We'll have it.'

'You're making an error,' said Gregor with finality as the waiter departed. 'You don't know how things work here.'

'Oh, don't exaggerate,' said Thrax. 'I ate fire for a living once. And I mean once.'

An odd hour was passed like a coded message as they learnt their worth in the eyes of the staff. Gregor was already in a semi-trance. He had slipped up somewhere. Society had finally caught up with him and thus he was condemned to be destroyed by a sort of hairless ape with a multitude of ears. He had expected it to happen eventually in one form or another – only the precise circumstances were a surprise.

'What's this crap I keep hearing about you thrusting your hips at a mirror?' the Beast Man asked him, trying to maintain the outward semblance of easy freedom in this oppressive place.

'I'm in love with myself, it's true.'

'Yourself.'

'Isn't that meant to be healthy? I've thrown away all my dummy cosmetics and dinosaur porn.'

When the meal arrived, it was a pig which seemed to have come to grief in a malarial swamp. Trailing from it was a padlock of fat, flash-fried in the cold sweat of years. A paper flag pronged into its hide warned: 'Those who free me never escape.'

'What's this?' asked the Beast Man.

'Something brought too soon from the incubator, by the look of it.'

'This is a meal?'

'Very much so. And a surprisingly expensive one.'

'Where are all the waiters?'

'Hiding. I *told* you how it would be.'

Looking at these seared relics, they devised a plan. Working as a team they could use the scalpel to hatch a few preliminary wounds and maybe scoop out the slime with apostle spoons. Then they would push the rest off the table and run.

But as they breached the torso they found that the entire thing was constructed of bucket pasta, painted with gravy. This was the last straw for the Beast Man. He found a waiter crouched behind the counter, sniggering into his hand. 'Get me the manager,' he told the startled employee, and the owner and master chef, Quandia Lucent, came out from the kitchen. Thrax gestured at the embryonic pasta hog. 'This meal is an obvious subterfuge – when's the real food coming?'

Perfectly composed, the chef raised an eyebrow. 'This is pasta, sir – consensus chow.'

'This is a joke, right?'

'Perhaps sir is a philistine,' Lucent responded dryly. 'With a glass tongue. One cannot put a price on pasta.'

'You do, every day.'

'I am initiated into the mysteries. "Without feast, no cruelty" is the chefs' credo. Food poisoning is the one constant throughout history. Is this round friend of yours the gentleman who smashed our front window with his hips, by any chance?'

'Don't try to change the subject to that unfortunate reality.'

'If sir is blind to the charms of slimy flour, perhaps sir would prefer the Carcinia Platelet, a medley of mushrooms in—'

'*Damn* your mushroom medley – such plunder and invention, yet no custard? We're getting out of here before our gorges rise and storm the freezer.'

Gregor followed Thrax out of the restaurant, leaving behind the dead and others who weren't so lucky. 'I told you, a cabinet fiend advises the chefs,' he reminded the Beast Man as they emerged into the square. 'Let's go to the cakeworks over there.' As they wandered over, he asked the Beast Man about the metal cross which hung about his neck. 'What is it? A key to something?'

'I think it used to be, but it's been copied and recopied so many times, a copy of a copy and so on, a million times, I suspect it's changed too much to open anything now.'

They entered the baker's and the proprietor asked after Gregor's wellbeing.

'Quickly my stomach increases, the trial of doctors,' said Gregor lustily, then asked for jackal cake.

The proprietor shook his head sadly. 'No demand, señor. Which is a shame, because people come in here and ask for it all the time.'

'Exactly, and it's advertised everywhere.'

'Propaganda is buried in the greatest desirability, señor,' said the drooping baker. 'Look at the crazy new gears on this fondant creation.'

'Controls on a bun?' the Beast Man queried.

'Young people don't care, señor,' sighed the baker. 'They live for craziness.'

'Well, as Bingo Violaine said,' the Beast Man smiled, ' "Man's arse is a despised necessity." '

'Come on out, Beast Man!' came a voice from outside. Looking through the display window, Thrax and Gregor saw five Followers of the Cannon in the street, flexing their gobs to emit sounds. 'Come out of that cakeshop and face your crimes against the one true religion!'

'Isn't chomping a religion?'

'Chomping? Are you all right, Beast Man?'

'I'm on top of the world. And chomping, yes, I'm sure of it. Chomp, chomp, I'm a better man. Oh the beauty's almost unbearable.'

'You transgress against the holy cannon by your secular antics! Is it not enough that we cannot find our murdered master's remains to fire unto the heavens? While your new friend Gregor acts like he's got a playground in his pocket?'

The baker opened a panel in the side wall and urged Gregor through it. 'Fools mean trouble, señor – heart pounding, blown up lungbags, not good for man or beast.'

Gregor found himself in the darkness of Donna Greeley's furniture store. All the furniture here was joined up into one big unwieldy piece which no one could move or afford. It had never been sold and the store had fallen into disuse. Greeley herself had died and dried out long ago, and Gregor felt leery of the dim carcass propped in the shadows. The Beast Man crawled in after him just before the front door burst open and the cannonites entered.

One of the benefits of having a heart like an ancient boiled sweet, Karloff reflected as he strolled under the sparred sky of the town square, is that when you see a strongman and a prizefighter being dragged out of a furniture shop and beaten up by a handful of priests, you don't react rashly. Enjoying a small cigar, Karloff watched the fight with interest.

He looked on till Cheney appeared beside him. 'What's the score, boss?'

'Examine well this boneless striver, Cheney. Our new boxer, I mean. Compound extremists came out in a rush, months away from satisfaction. Religion is not candid. Smug dozens don't see both ways. Yet he looked at the anger and bungled his response. Tried a begging gambit.'

'Begging?'

'And weeping. The Beast Man also.'

'A weeping gambit's good for embarrassing the opponent.'

'Well it didn't this time. The Fuseheads just stood there. First Round realised after a while his attackers had selected a basic staring gambit, so he stopped. Then the priests attacked them both anew.'

'How'd the victims respond?'

'With a bleeding and blacking-out gambit – and that's where you came in. Our so-called "Masked Inconvenience" has been unconscious in the dust for ten minutes now. I think I see how the land lies with that one.'

'I got the gun,' said Cheney.

'Ah,' sighed the Fall Marshall. 'As Violaine said, "Even an illusion is made from the real." I should get some practice in.'

Mayor Rudloe pushed back the hood of his containment suit, removed his Jonathan glasses and looked nervously about the striped operating tent. Against a tragedy-stained backdrop stood the Fall Marshall, the red stripes of his glass hat corkscrewing ever to the sky. Behind angled aluminium bars paced a tiger striped like a zebra, its movement creating moray patterns. 'Ah, this is what it's all about, eh?' asked Rudloe uncertainly.

Dietrich ducked in behind the Mayor.

'You can tell the wingding to get lost,' said Karloff.

'Who?'

'The paravamp. *Ave tyrannis.*'

Dietrich raised the crust of an eyebrow. 'You seem to know a lot about it.' He turned and went out.

'Never mind that method-acting demon of yours,' said Karloff, messing with some equipment. 'We are an itinerant collective and in this world that means swift travel via other realms – our arrivals are unwelcome enough without our trailing clouds of poison effluvia from the mainlands. So the creepchannel is convenient, but I rarely pause to have dealings with demons.'

'A rather lengthy denial about something I don't remotely understand. And what's this?' The Mayor picked something off the ground.

'The Chestnut of Death.'

'*God* almighty!' Rudloe threw the nut away in a puff of goofer dust. 'I've serious reservations about this three-ring circus you call a . . . circus.'

'You upper classes – so at home in a vacuum you can find three syllables in it. Bite into doubt, you'll find good reason. You'll end undone and sliding down bath mirror steam, Mayor.'

'Well, it's true that being petitioned by ghastly scum is not all it's cracked up to be. The hairpin turns of m'policies have left my mind scratched to oblivion, really. No thought can travel smoothly across it any more. Maybe you've got the right idea, living out of your hat. Midden freaks and no traceable premises – that's probably the stuff.'

'Yes, my pleasure in gain displayed as entertainment, for a

hefty charge – immaculate profit, I think you'll agree.' Karloff took what looked like a length of twisted bone from a carved wooden box. 'Do you know what this is?'

'A measure of your desperation?'

A middle-of-the-range clown entered in funny duds and makeup.

'The recent unpleasantness of our performance is to be repeated,' the Fall Marshall continued. 'And since Chance Macabre now has a pressing engagement with some maggots, I must take up his act. Just as the illusionist relies on misdirection, living the clown's life is a simple thing if you exaggerate your legs and cover your face in shame. This bright-eyed, saucy little gun is a product of the white heat of technology. When I fire, Brit Hume here will catch the bullet in his teeth.'

'The white heat of my arse more like! That's the Wesley Kern gun!'

Karloff aimed the gun at the glum smile of Hume, and fired. The head of mushroom flesh exploded, the clown dropping like a sack of worms. Rudloe rushed up and stared aghast at the corpse as Karloff briskly wiped the pistol.

'I thought you said he'd catch the bullet in his teeth.'

'He did – as you can plainly see.'

'I suppose I misunderstood your claim.'

'Once again,' said Karloff, replacing the gun in the ornate case. 'Misdirection. No real loss – dualistic thought's been cranking out clowns for centuries. Now let's see if we can't rehearse a similar act with you, Mr Mayor.'

'I'll battle it all the way to the wire,' gasped Rudloe.

'But your stone bald misrule requires such occasional charm offensives.'

'On condition I survive!' shouted Rudloe.

A silver-painted midget with eyes black as seeds entered the tent, skidding in slurry and quickly righting himself.

'This is my assistant, Mayor – Halliburton-Hussein Cheney.'

'The one who put his soul into a worm family?'

The midget ignored him. 'Message from the target, Mr Velocet. He's putting the entire crap axis on the Masked Inconvenience. Winner takes all, angel and animals.'

'You're joking.'

'I'm telling you what he said.'

Karloff gave a delighted, astonished bark of laughter. 'Tell him I accept.'

'And that new zombie's scaring the riggers.'

'Excellent. Did you see how Fang threw himself into it? A putrescent streak a mile wide, that one. Skeleton makes good. Those demised daredevils were incomplete without him. I heard there was an incident with one of the Iscariot beetles you got from Del.'

'One of the saddles slid and a kid became entangled in some legs like black scissors. Oh, and that shyster mug wants to see you.'

Max Gaffer stormed into the tent, his head-swords slashing slits in the canopy.

'I thought you were dead,' said the Mayor.

'Sure, dead like a fox!'

'Metal visor nailed directly into your face, eh? Can't say I'm entirely surprised. And those swords look awkward.'

'They are.'

'So you know this hen-in-waiting too, Karloff?' Rudloe asked the Fall Marshall.

'Who better to liaise with criminals than a bungling brimstone-bandit?' And Karloff turned to the lawyer to bark, 'Well, what is it? Speak up, man!'

'I delivered – it's your turn.'

'My heart falls open like a pocketwatch, Gaffer, and gives you a few minutes. What a pity that isn't enough. I'm dangling my gratitude your way – in the form of some liver, look.' Karloff pulled some meat from his coat and flung it at the lawyer's feet.

'Liver? I did what I promised. Two positives can't make a negative.'

'Yeah, right. I promised that the consequences would be aimed at someone else and so they will. That's politics after all, eh?'

Gaffer pounded his forehead with the heels of his palms, spluttering as his hands were lacerated. 'What – what's . . . ?'

'You take yourself too seriously, Maximillion. More seriously than I take you, or the Mayor here. That set chin and gleaming eyes of yours won't make any difference, I'm afraid. They're rubbish to me. You see, even among clowns there's a limit. Your rotted-out motivations appal everybody. You've made a pig's ear of this, haven't you? As above, so below.'

'You know about that?'

'Your position with Sweeney? That you're the office plunger? I have absolute confidence your every ambition will end at the base of a cliff. Cheney, take it outside.'

The midget plunged his head into Gaffer's belly, pedalling his legs so that the demi-demon was forced backward out of the tent, tears like worms dangling from its eyes.

'Now,' resumed Karloff, 'where were we? Ah yes, calamitous mayhem and insane megalomania.'

But before they could continue, the Beast Man entered, looking roughed-up and apologetic. 'I've come to tender my resignation, Mr Velocet.'

'Oh really? Well that's an awful shame.'

'It's the pure evil, Mr Velocet – it's just not me. I hope this won't inconvenience you.'

'I always knew you'd become a townie, Dugway,' laughed Karloff good-naturedly. 'Go off with you, and no hard feelings, eh?'

'Thank you, Mr Velocet.' And the Beast Man ducked out.

'Shame about old Dugway, he's a sweet man despite his Popeye arms. Wears that carmencross because it's an infinity compass containing every detail. You can bet a reindeer doesn't know that. Not really surprised he threw in the sponge.'

'I don't want to hear about this bizarre world of sponges,

liver and reindeer you inhabit!' shouted the Mayor. 'What's this nonsense about shooting me in the face?'

'Oh, no need for that now – you'll be replacing the Beast Man.'

'Being shot out of a cannon?'

'It doesn't often happen the other way around, and what if it did? It's like a man swallowing fire – evens the score.'

'What's this crazy talk?'

'Minutes black as ants as you wait for the blast. When midday hurtles at you for the first time, you'll love it.'

'What then?'

'You'll be found months later, fool's-parsley growing through your ribcage.'

By the time the Mayor returned to his office he felt inchoate, all volition gone, like a man plucked this way and that by a tailor. He fell into his seat with a gasp and sat resembling almost exactly the portrait behind him, in which he looked like a lump of scorched dough. He was about to clang his eyelids when Max Gaffer flung into the room, followed by an apologetic Dietrich. 'I grabbed hold of him, sir, but he's so slimy . . .'

'I know, I know. What do you want, Gaffer?'

'Is that all you have to say?'

'No, I'd like to thank you – your troubles are an ore-body I mine for glee. Your downfall's been a marvel to watch. Has a mistake ever been so precise at such a speed? I'd like to shake your hand and stop awkwardly for a photo.'

'Don't be absurd.'

'So you tried a task in your exile – was the result of any worth? Your head's ribbed and flavoured, are you satisfied?'

'No,' said Max Gaffer, exhaling his anger and sitting down miserably. 'I'm treated like a makeweight down there, over there. Cold hell. Sweeney regards m'lying skills as child's play.'

'The world of grief is not always one of participation,' Dietrich chipped in.

'What does that mean?'

'I mean it's inescapable. Grief is.'

Gaffer looked at Dietrich with slow scorn. 'You demons. It's just hog heaven for you round here, isn't it?'

'You're a demon yourself, Max,' Rudloe pointed out. 'What are those pulsing lugs in your throat?'

'Shrike-filters.'

'Well there you go, a demon. So what do you want?'

'Treason is pliant. I want you to take me back.'

'Are you hearing this, Dieter? He wants to come back. Used to walk around with ears instead of warrants.'

'And now I've got warrants for ears, so what?'

'Does all shame cease under the Planck length?'

'Bet your life it does. It's unbeatable.'

'Stop saying that, Max.'

'What?'

'"Unbeatable." That privilege is no longer yours. I refuse to take your request seriously. Dietrich here barely knows what human beings are and even he's better liked than you – people wave at him in the street, throw babies at him, everything.'

'Flowers,' Dietrich added.

'Give him flowers and so on. You? Obsessed with your underwear, your time in this office was a monsoon of unparalleled depravity. Unprecedented criticism was voiced of your buttocks, both separately and together. You're not telling me such flak was unfounded. So here you are finally, toppled and confessed. Even that ringmaster won't have you.'

'He's a fool – thinks he can teach tricks to a Steinway spider.'

'Eh? Steinways you say?'

'With whip and piano stool.'

'I don't believe you – you'll say anything at this point. Maybe you should go see doomed Eddie Gallo. Squeaking of rights and freedoms, he snips his scissors at the rain. You and he deserve each other.'

Gaffer stood abruptly, knocking his chair over backwards. '*My* performance in vice is unassailable, punctuated as it is by regular betrayal. But you? You're a limb on the Conglomerate. As Violaine said: "Cheap harm lasts just as long."' And he stormed out of the room, his head-swords slashing chips from the doorframe.

'Send out the Brigade,' the Mayor told Dietrich, 'to keep the clowns in line. And I don't like this notion of rogue pianos.'

Never one to waste a bit of rotting meat, Karloff took the liver into his wagon and slapped it on to the table, closing the door and sitting down. From a drawer he took a thin black spine resembling barbed wire and pushed it into the glossy congestion so that it stood like an antenna. Rewiring mercy nerves in the face of this hepatic conduit, he recited a credo which ended with the words, 'Reform changes the shape of injustice.' The searing grey drone of creepchannel flux leaked sour light from the forensic transmitter. Migraine bile scrambled up the trailer walls as Karloff was filled with a dirty vacuum.

'Quit griping or whatever that noise is,' said the demon Sweeney, its voice fluttering against the crackle of the underworld. 'I need hardly remind you that I purchased your rapacious handiwork for fifty large and an agreement not to snip your nose off – tee hee! How's Accomplice?'

'Species of bark are given names. Bugs cross the face of a barn in less than an hour – fact. And the front of the heads have eyes now.'

'They have had for a long time, haven't they?'

Karloff thought about it. 'Yes, I suppose they have. And their customs, compared to elsewhere . . . One more bit of etiquette and I swear the dead will return in exasperation.'

'Yes, "manners" – two laws look at each other. Press on anyway, eh? What was that?'

'Nothing. I was nodding in agreement.'

'Knobbing?'

'Nodding, I said. And watching a fist-sized tarantula going past.'

'Ah, that thick spindle of fear, the tarantula. I wish I was there to see it with you. If there was any animal I could fold up and put in my mouth I'd select the good old tarantula. Eating well?'

'Apple fritters.'

'Playing it safe, eh? Good. Is the massacre prepared?'

'Can't you tell?'

'I know only a centre of it, never all the details.'

'Well, I test-fired the gun and it's a peach. I have a false crisis planned for the purpose of subsequent complacency. And my cover is perfect. In the ring I load standard wonders into their vacant faces. I float by my comrades as ever, dispensing aspersions like an ecclesiast. Horror is expected, and horror it shall be.'

'I told you the possession of their cultural icons would give you even greater hypnotic power. I await the influx of graves. Enough jawing.'

'OK. Here I go.'

Karloff unpicked the radio, kicked open the wagon door and threw it to a dog.

7

Octopus

Damnation – it takes as long as it takes

The Flying Dead Brothers ascended the Tower of Nowt in broad daylight, pieces of their skin dropping on to passers-by. Fang was stressed. 'Are you sure we're authorised to clamber up here?'

'Doctors are mermaids in their imagination,' called Squill.

'That's not what I asked. And wouldn't it be better to do this at night?'

'I'm laughing.'

'No you're not.'

'I would be if I weren't busy climbing. Hoop-la!' Squill swung on a dead flagpole through an upper window. He stuck his head out of the window again to shout, 'And put your weight behind it!' but his head fell away through space, smashing in the road.

The brain-hung Enrico muscled swiftly upward, hauling himself inside. When Fang joined him in the upper chamber, carrying the badly rotted Ladaat, the tower guard Murdster was stood there fully alert to their intrusion. He held a machete the colour of tar.

The hefty Enrico gaped in sick dismay, but Fang placed Ladaat carefully down and turned his custard head and canary-yellow eyes upon the sentinel. 'What course of exhaustion d'you favour, friend?'

'I pretend to be alert.'

'Where?'

'Here.'

'What do they pay a guard these days?'

'With carefully contrived documents of a threatening nature, bills of lading, and a shout upside the face.'

'I'm surprised. Nine French fries are usually adequate.'

With a yell, Murdster swung the blade and slashed Fang's arm from his shoulder.

Fang awaited some follow-up remark from the sentinel and, receiving none, gestured to his stump and asked, 'Well? Whattya mean?'

'Fang, the Rotten Star!' bellowed Enrico and when Murdster turned to look at him, Fang kicked Ladaat from the floor. The torso hit Murdster full in the nose, knocking him backward over the headless Squill and through an opposite window.

'Is this it?' asked Fang, inspecting the length of fake-looking ham stretched between two pegs on a pedestal. 'The Moral Fibre?'

Enrico shook his head slowly and fiercely. 'I don't know, Fangy my brother. I *just don't know.*'

Ladaat piped up from the floor, 'Remember what the Fall Marshall said: "Bring back that little beauty from the Tor Magdala or you'll never fly again." '

Fang frowned. 'And what Bingo Violaine said. "Consensus is reality with the crusts cut off." '

The lawyer Max Gaffer wandered over to the canyon edge where doomed Eddie Gallo was crouching quietly on the stumped flyover with a hammer and a length of wood.

Doomed Eddie Gallo looked up slowly and carefully. His cardigan flapped and cracked in the wind. 'Hello, Max Gaffer,' he whispered. 'These are planks newly sawn from the Awkward Forest. Boy, the trouble I had. They've got keys to the trees round there. And I suspect they are constantly stealing the wood back.' A sloth appeared from behind a buckled nugget of concrete and began creeping slowly toward him. He regarded the sloth sadly. 'I'd like to sit on those things. But I daren't.'

The sloth exploded suddenly, knocking doomed Eddie Gallo backward into a hedge on terra firma. He seemed to be laughing.

This is what I've come to, thought Gaffer.

Wise old heifers gazed at the scene, and then at each other.

Gaffer went over and helped the mayoral candidate out of the bushes. 'How goes the mayoral campaign, doomed Eddie Gallo?'

'I carve lovely hearts from bits of turnip and throw them out the window of a car,' whispered doomed Eddie Gallo. 'One hit an old gran in the eye and she sued me to within an inch of my life, screeching and pointing all the time. That got me a lot of press, as you can imagine.'

Gaffer wasn't surprised. This idiot had once made a mini-ature sculpture of his own head and shoulders from white bread. 'Why are you whispering, doomed Eddie Gallo?'

'Am I? I can't hear a thing. Too many sloth explosions. I mainly look these days. Yesterday my attention was captured by a high thing which moved in air-knocking motion.'

Gaffer smacked dust from doomed Eddie Gallo's clothes and yelled in his ear, 'You mean you saw a bird!'

'Bird? I suppose it was. Something different about you, Max Gaffer. A haircut?'

'I've been modified into a sort of demi-demon, doomed Eddie Gallo! Look at me!'

'Eh?'

'Demon, I said! Swords in my head! See?'

'Ah!'

'Swords! And the Church of Automata hammered this bridle into my cheeks!'

'Bridle? Ah, I see, a sort of metal mask. The day has left your trouble swollen, eh?'

'Yes!'

They sat down among duct stones, ear weeds and cactus skeletons.

'I'd like to help with your mayoral campaign, doomed Eddie Gallo! I of course put Rudloe where he is today!'

'Oh? I heard you were running on fumes.'

'Wha—? Well that's as may be, but I can give you a fair shake at it! For instance, how many rich tea biscuits have you eaten today?'

'No more than two or three thousand.'

'That's what I'm talking about! Look at the politics, doomed Eddie Gallo, what it's all about! King Verbal could boneseed a bridge here with ease – but would he personally see that as progress? He's got himself quite a set-up, after all!'

Gallo's face lit up, then became puzzled. 'Yes, I suppose he could. These are our tall poppy days, our salad days – ever put tall poppies in a salad? The stalks push your cheeks out like a tent.'

'Don't zone out on me, doomed Eddie Gallo! I think you're on to something with this canyon crossing stunt! But you have to be practical! And "Bless the ultimate strangeness" is not a campaign slogan!'

'Oh I've a back-up plan, Max Gaffer, never fear – look. Gull glue, from the Shop of a Thousand Spiders. Found it between the blood glass and the cannibal cigarettes. My tin friend Maquette is working there with that scary boy. With this application, I won't have to hammer and disturb those sloths.'

Gaffer looked at the tube of glue which doomed Eddie Gallo had handed him:

Ingredients: rogue lard; negative flake (15%); some kind of stringy ectoplasmic snot from the muzzle of a jagged old crone whose better days exist only in her mind; aqua; colouring (mole-pearl, E171); tears; vulture shadow; daisies (95%); modified starch; carnauba wax.

As the lawyer finished the list, someone kicked into his ribs, falling on top of him. The trickster Prancer Diego could never work out how to slow up before he reached people. 'An unfortunate incident, happily in the past,' Prancer chortled, thrashing among them. 'The problem is: aaaaaaaaah!'

'What's the *matter* with you?' Gaffer choked.

'I'm growing ten individual species of nostril lizards.'

'Nostril lizards?'

Doomed Eddie Gallo laughed fit to burst. 'Ho ho! This fellow Prancer – a lot of gumption, eh Max Gaffer?'

Closing his eyes, Max Gaffer finally shrugged off the encumbrance of hope.

Seeing everything through the added context of time, the Abblatia angel saw his cage as a tiny barcode, a barely noticeable detail amid green battlements sparkling in rain, orchards cut and bleeding summer into coffee earth, branches underground laden with coral rinds and deep-packed stairs of old empire. Light, flowers and immense material, a realm of zooming fire. The cage was in fact only five days wide, and elsewhere Abblatia visited Spacey's Gas Station to find Barny Juno looking at a car covered in radiator backblow and semi-obliterated decals.

'Hello Mike Abblatia,' Barny said. 'This thing needs plugging with muscle junk and etheric shielding. Penny rhino on the dash and spoiler adornments like sovereign rings. Couldn't wake Dot.'

Abblatia gladly worked with Barny on the car a while, fitting it with a narrow goofer tank, a soapstone dashboard and an old carpet which had absorbed creepchannel leakage from a previous roof and was sprouting tough mushrooms. They were just callibrating new palladium valves to the suicide clutch when Chloe Low walked by and Barny asked her if she'd seen the fight.

'There you go again,' Chloe sighed. 'With your animals.'

'Not just that – my house is disappearing.'

Doctor Perfect hove up in front of Abblatia, his long spatulate fingers spindling like a spider. 'Gold bones? How did he arrive at this condition?'

Karloff Velocet was stood with the doctor atop a scaffold, looking through Abblatia's cage bars. 'Some sort of progress glowing beyond its size.'

'Change without needles – that's objectionable.'

'So is anything without profit, surely, for a corpse artisan?'

'I won't deny it. Well, I don't see what you want me to do here. I suspect it's simply been re-forgotten so many times it's been allowed into its own sidespace.'

'I was just curious. You're available for the fight tonight?'

'Of course. Doctors do not want for purpose – they want for one they can achieve. I'll bring some of my famous knives.'

The doctor lived in stethoscope darkness, ignoring the condition of his cigarette heart.

Brimming in the poison yolk of his throne, Sweeney called down the Ruby Aspict as creatures of blown ghost sifted in and out of the walls, reciting laws and raising their eyebrows ironically. The Sawvillian protocol demon Rammstein kicked through some black ice buds which had been born dead to the yellowed frost of hell. Every atom here had jaws, gnawing at life's feeble push. The biomechanical king demon peered down from its leathery half shell. 'I'm checking up on old Trouble Trubshaw, Rammy. He should be well into mischief by now. Let's take a peek into this harebrained scheme they call the miracle of creation.'

Everything would be seen in red, a fever window. The fleshy gemstone turned, a dented heaven dark in its depths. Then appeared broken-down gardens, cored cars, slang vines and Vonn Stropp crows. 'Well we know he's in the right place, at least.'

But the scene which next appeared showed Trubshaw belting away at a heavy punch-bag, sweat flying off him. At his back Karloff Velocet shouted, 'Carry on that slow you'll become a byword for soil, boy!'

'So regret me,' Trubshaw growled.

'What did he say?' Sweeney asked.

Rammstein was embarrassed. 'It's in an unfamiliar dialect, Your Majesty.'

'That big lug of a demon, what's he doing?'

'Nothing useful, that's for sure. Genius is like a pause – transplant it and it loses meaning.'

'Trubshaw's not a genius, he's just a bastard, a thug.'

'Then perhaps he's in the right place after all.'

'What's he punching? Barny Juno better be in that bag.'

But Trubshaw was now snoozing peacefully in the shade of bitter apples.

'What's Juno doing?'

The Aspict switched to a view of Barny leaning on a lion's head and looking at his partly disassembled house.

'What about that frayed exclamation mark, what's his name: Edge. Plantin Edge – show him!'

A ripple passed through the Aspict, revealing a tree the living green of lizards. Beneath it, standing in tropical cotton and car-tyre sandals, Edgy was slowly moving a placid hen through the air as if it flew. A fierce woman snapped at him, 'You only just woke up?'

'For my part, new days are nothing. I always crouch in my shirt. Don't try to change me, baby.'

The girl stood staring point-blank into Edgy's face. 'Don't make me come over there, Palatino.'

'What about the hen?'

'Get rid of it!' snapped the demon Sweeney.

'He can't hear you, Lord,' said Rammstein.

'I was dismissing the Aspict!' Sweeney roared as the ruby cleared. He sat back, fulminating. 'It's like a recurring dream which I can't affect. Why was Karloff urging Trubshaw to punch some sort of huge sausage?'

'A mere formality, perhaps.'

'In any case, Plan A and B have collided. I can no longer depend on the efficiency of either.' Sweeney leaned forward and, bracing his many legs, began to tear himself from his throne. Sinews stretched, gas exploding from fluke-holes as Sweeney exposed a spine made of black gemstone. Torn rags leaked yellow acid. It was like a monstrous lobster wrenching itself from a trapped and useless tail. Muscles shut behind him, sealing, and he stood free in the freezing electric air. 'The life photo uncorks and I'm with them, my sharp chin in their shoulder. The implications are bleak, eh? Above I go! Ha ha! If there could have been more moments like this!'

Passing walls like a scald, Sweeney heaved from the cavern and the beating of his coldwater heart faded away.

As Rammstein stood bathed in the rubine saturation of the blanked Aspict, he gazed toward the towering bloody socket of the Emperor's throne.

8

It's Your Funeral

Fear is not a real baby

Squared off in his containment suit, Mayor Rudloe walked across the soft collagen floor of the extraction shed's basement. Bloody ropes and knots of greed hung from the ceiling and cancer curds like rotting fruit marshed the walls around Old Gory. The Conglomerate, a biocracy of sloshing bodies joined in an alimentary morass, whispered among themselves, 'Remember poor old option twenty.'

Rudloe coughed to gain their attention and a few turret mouths projected from the mass. 'Mr Rudloe,' said one. 'How goes the long con?'

'M'jurisdiction is shimmering before me. And I've a new campaign slogan – "My Pelvis is Grand".'

'It's rubbish.'

Rudloe grimaced. 'I know.'

'Anything else?'

'I found some snot on the stair rail. Oh, and someone stole the Moral Fibre again, the new rubber version. I think this time I'll use some sort of hard plastic, so long as it looks right. A cheap pink shoe-horn or something, I think I've got one in the drawer.'

One slubby mouth asked another, 'This antique shock regarding the Fibre – does it really operate?'

'No, it's just traditional. Its function is primarily to distract and waste time, like the circus. Speaking of which, how's that going, Rudloe?'

'Eh?' Rudloe had been stepping carefully around some intestinal links. 'Oh, it's all anyone can talk about. And dogs, of course.'

'Dogs are talking about the circus?'

'People are talking about dogs.'

Another mouth piped up, 'The citizenry certainly know how to have a good time. We trust that your token show of mayhem in the ring will not imply you've anything but sham originality at your disposal.'

'I guarantee you that all will attend the levy. That my show of being folksy is understood by everyone to be mere pretence. I met a farmer the other day and tried to convince him I was a fine fella. He wasn't having any of it.'

'How are you sure?'

'How? His disbelief was expressed facially, if you really want to know. All right? His features could barely keep up with each other in the stampede toward incredulity. In fact you'll be pleased to hear that acts of complete disregard have reached record figures. They understand that there is a threat to them, behind our blithe shite. You know, I suspect I could tell them the whole truth? And nothing would happen.'

'They already know it – and either pretend otherwise or that they approve. That's what participation is, and why you can't truly call them victims. D'you think anyone's really dumb enough not to know?'

'I suppose not.'

'Ructions occur only at a transition – if everyone already knows they are powerless, what's to adjust to? We expect a fine extraction this year.'

The demons Dietrich and Gettysburg had a room in the observatory. Their window was an auxiliary observation blister facing the sea. 'Is that a new house out there?' asked

Gettysburg, peering out with strange pearlite eyes. 'Near the Announcement Horse?'

'Can't be – it would have to be in the sea.'

'This is Accomplice. They'd build houses in their ears if they thought it would help them avoid some sort of blame.'

Dietrich shook his heavy head. 'There's still so much I don't know.' He turned away from the domed window and sat in a boneseed armchair. 'I mean, I've settled in all right. I've got a black breastplate, a head like an anchor – what's not to love?'

The white and winged Getty stood against the blaze of the window, a silhouette with laser eyes. 'I agree, obviously.'

'But I think they assume I'm so fascinated by human beings that if certain laws were repealed I'd immediately begin killing one. Well I don't mind. If necessary I'll forgive them by brute force. There's no place for me below any more, even if I wanted it. You know Sweeney's promoted Rammy to my station?'

'The Ponce? He's not captain material.'

'I know.' Dietrich looked through several walls at the old astronomer who sat in the central chamber. Then he turned back to the dazzling demon. 'How was it when *you* defected?'

'I sprung out all aglee, and banged against a hell hound – not what I wanted.'

'I can imagine.'

'I didn't really know what to do, once I got here. I decided to cackle in slants of illuminated dust. Old habits die hard.'

'Well, the hordes of Satan need something to do,' Dietrich conceded encouragingly. 'It's been a tough stretch for the hordes.'

'Anyway, in the end I had to remind myself what brought me here.' Getty gestured to Bingo Violaine's lower jaw which was fixed to a wooden plaque on the wall.

Dietrich sat forward. 'You too? You never told me that.'

'Yes. So I plunged finally inside the minutes. What did

Violaine say? "A virtuous path in the world doesn't cease to function, it's just obscured." '

'Yeah, but a path obscured ceases to function.'

'Hmm . . . you're right. That's what I love – between scorn and dry laughter, you really mean it.'

'You remember what he said in *The Hive of Heaven*? "Nature is not murdered without a consequent haunting. A lesson may be learnt. Yet some bodies take medicine as a reproach." '

Some sort of gilled carrot with big eyes crawled across the outside of the window, claiming their attention briefly.

'Anyway, Violaine may be the best of them,' Dietrich continued. 'But we still disagree on this. You think these people are angels; I came here because humanity's way more evil than anything below, our vaudeville villainy.' Dietrich scratched the rust on his chin, looking aside. 'At least, the manipulators are.'

Gettysburg was suddenly alert. 'A little more than you realised,' he said. 'And monotonous. Unimaginative.'

'Yes,' said Dietrich, shifting a little uncomfortably. 'At close quarters, I find myself accessory to worse evils than any Sweeney asked of me. I confess the un-officed characters around here are more interesting, though they're collaborators.'

Gettysburg could hardly believe it. He frowned, happy. 'You're going to quit.'

'Maybe I am.'

Dietrich stood and deployed the window, his leather wings stretching open, and soon two demons were in full sail, miles high and ducking clouds.

The Brigade entered the forest, the Sarge's uptilted face immediately cooled by dappled leafshade. It was still hot, though late afternoon. 'Ah, lads, it gave me a fine and special feeling when I went before the disciplinary committee. Very quickly they had had a bellyful. "Give me ten half-decent soldiers," I told them, "and I'll give you five decent ones. I have glue." Ha, ha – that's the stuff to give 'em. And now duty forces us to intrude into the Awkward Forest, a lot of which seems to have been sawn down by clowns.'

'I saw a cartoon of clowns sawing at trees, Sarge. Years ago. They did the same movement over and over, all quivery and with big eyes. I was really scared.'

'Scared of an old cartoon, Gibbs? What's that paper, what are you about now?'

'Translating poetry, Sarge – *Four Sky Code*, from the Kraut. And Perkins here is illustrating it with pictures of birds in their glory.'

'I can draw birds,' said the cadet, showing the Sarge a sketch of a frog.

'That's not a bird, Perkins – it's a canyon tree frog. It's good, though. Doesn't he look as if he existed in that crevice? That's because his rough skin provides a bark-like camouflage.' He indicated the foliage detail. 'The main virtue of these flowers is that they are not and never will be our last resort in battle.' The Sarge chuckled to himself. 'Imagine that, though. Flowers.' Chuffed, he turned to his Deputy, who brandished a dish.

'Snail, Sarge?'

'Don't mind if I do. What are they?'

'Snails, Sarge.'

'Snails. Don't mind if I do.'

'Get your face round that then.'

'What is it.'

'A snail, Sarge.'

'Snail. All right then. Eat it do I?'

'Eat it Sarge, that's right.'

'What is it.'

'Snail – a snail, Sarge.'

'Snail.'

'A snail, Sarge. See? It's a snail.'

'Snail is it. Well now.'

'Snail.'

'Snail, eh. Well, don't mind if I do.'

'Good on yuh.'

'Right.'

'You eatin' it then?'

'Eh?'

'You eatin' that?'

'What is it.' Before the Deputy could reply, the Sarge fell into a ditch. 'On the face of it, I was careless. But only if you misunderstand what I intended to achieve. I managed to disturb a crow, which went whacking off into the upper canopy. There's a lesson in that, eh Perkins?'

'I understand, Sarge.'

The rest of the troops jumped into the ditch, disturbing dozens of crows.

9

How Some People Adjust

When every channel shows the same picture,
you know it's something you should ignore

On the way into the fight tent, Barny asked B.B. Henrietta if she'd seen Gregor anywhere: 'I went to his basement. Pillow sprats and dust monkeys, that's all I found.' Dust monkeys were formed when corner dust became so dense it began to develop a limb structure and started capering awkwardly about.

'Playing pocket billiards in a vat of dough, for all I care,' B.B. replied, and they joined Edgy in the wooden seats around the ring. There was a stall crowded with dried clenched fists and false animals made of greasy wrought iron for kids to hug and cherish. Stampede Door-to-Door had paid for ad space around the ring, with shouts for products such as Exploding Bridal Gowns, Dismle (the Dismal Trifle), Stern Greeting Cards, Edible Embers and Britch Biscuits – 'just pop 'em in the washing machine and in no time at all your clothes will disintegrate'. In a corner of the ring, the withered corpse of an old lady was propped in a wicker chair.

Disguised in the audience, the Mayor and Dietrich Hammerwire conferred. 'Makes a change from crab races,' muttered the Mayor.

'And headless darts.'

'Headless you say?' the Mayor replied with fulsome disinterest, frowning past the ring.

On the other side a media commotion was headed by Douglas Bar of the Douglas Bar Show, whose oily mouth was saying 'Where's my undying driver?' and 'Tonight defies observation or analysis, I'll need mints' and 'Shove my broadcast on the air, my mirth is priceless, last night I taught nobody, tonight I'll offer independence.' Then he shoved a microphone at Karloff Velocet, who sat in the front row. 'Mr Velocet, tell me about yourself.'

'Which appalling legend do you want to hear?'

'It's said that you had to be coaxed and persuaded to put on such a savage fight.'

'I was approached three times. First time I indicated a banana, second time I indicated a river.'

'Was this intended as a negative?'

'No, I like both those things and I wanted them combined together at last.'

'And here comes the Masked Inconvenience. This balloon, as it seems easiest to term him, wears a black woollen mask yet seems to flinch whenever anyone approaches him.' Bar pushed through the crowd to the masked Gregor. 'Mr Inconvenience, how do you feel about your chances?'

'Life hasn't been kind to me. Dogged by bad luck, I'm also an idiot.'

'And how have you spent the crucial twelve hours before the fight?'

'I decided to pet a cat and the animal looked reconciled to the prospect, so we embarked upon that ordeal together.'

Frowning, Karloff Velocet snipped a Zippo at the underside of a plastic tulip. 'Shall we get on?'

Bar took his place at the commentator's table with the hated Rooster as Gregor crawled through the ropes and stood droopy in the spotlight. Rooster bent to the mike. 'Hello and welcome to the Tar Baby Concerns. We're here at the fight of the year, something I haven't really got a clue about, I freely admit. Time me, Jim, as I look from one end of the ring to the other.'

'That took four seconds, Rooster, the way you did it. And my name's not Jim. It's Douglas Bar speaking, with the hated Rooster as we attempt to remain civilised before an audience of raging primitives. The champion Trubshaw versus the Masked Inconvenience. Put on your Jonathan glasses, everyone – this'll be a blinder, sponsored as it is by Stampede Products, "The firm that flirts with danger". And here's the Fall Marshall to announce the losers.'

Karloff Velocet took to the ring and hailed the participants. 'In the red corner, stern and showing it, that mountain of muscle and infernodyne innards, a head with its own microclimate and a pluck of hair like the true bastard – a man who pronounces "stegosaurus" as a single-syllable word – Trubshaw!'

The demon Trubshaw lumbered out of the shadows, its ears cleaned and armour buffed to high polish. Its face was way, way smaller than its head, as though rubber-stamped on the front of it. Gregor began sobbing as the crowd cheered.

'And in the blue corner, weighing more than anyone should, breathing beyond his means, sobbing like a child and already quite shaky on his pins – the challenger, the Masked Inconvenience!'

The crowd threw dried clenched fists and false animals made of greasy wrought iron at Gregor.

'It's fish against fowl,' cried Karloff, 'a war as groundless and profitable as ever there were. To your corners!'

Karloff vacated the ring and Gregor staggered to his corner, where his cornerman Thrax tried to wring tears from the woolly mask without revealing Gregor's identity.

Douglas Bar and Rooster were drawing excitement from empty air. 'Rumour has it,' stated Rooster, 'that the Masked Inconvenience has made little effort to research his opponent's strategy and exercised not at all.'

'If so, this young man is about to reap the whirlwind of his lethargy. Unless he takes the precaution of smashing his legs in the opening minutes of the fight—'

'His own legs, Jim?'

'Any two of the six legs out there, if broken, would make a difference to this battle. Both fighters are fairly shapeless and we must assume they know it. This masked fellow, after his own fashion, is a human being. His opponent, by contrast, looks slightly demonic, what with the claws and many ears.'

'Could be trained in the supernatural assault tradition, Jim. He lives from the fist outward. It's said he refuses to remove his gum shield during conversation.'

'I heard he was born with one already in place. One thing's for sure – it won't be any dance around the maypole for the Mask. As our great philosopher said, "Real suffering is not a spectacle for philosophers – too messy." '

'He also said, "Only a spectator may inherit the riches of war – participants merely pick over the lessons." I don't understand either quote and the subject bores me. The ref tonight is the dead Donna Greeley of Greeley's furniture store, and there's the bell.'

Gregor cringed across the tattooed floor toward the glittering monster. Trubshaw was instantly lamping him one around the belly.

'A right hook to the belly,' shouted Bar, 'knocking it aside. But the rest of the masked man's body structure remains in place and Trubshaw can only stand and wait while the belly slows down and resettles into place. We're waiting too. Trubshaw's gloves are in flamingo leather, by the way. And the masked man's gloves are giraffe velvet. Well, the belly has stopped and the Masked Inconvenience is drooping forward like a flower. He looks pale, like a mime hit by lightning. And Trubshaw delivers a deadly uppercut to his primary chin and the challenger's head snaps back, sending twenty-seven beads of sweat into the air. He staggers backward, crossing the floor with what reason insists must be his legs.'

'My skeleton! My skeleton!' screamed Gregor.

'And the masked man is screaming about his skeleton, it

seems he's having trouble with it. He shields his forehead and thinks he's hidden. But the beefy Trubshaw can see the stout and fretful figure well enough. Mr Inconvenience chooses to slump in the rigging with arms hung quivering in the breach, I kid you not, just flapping in the breeze. As Trubshaw approaches with only one decision to make: whether to punch his lights out or measure him up for a nightgown. And there's the bell – I could barely hear it above another rending, wailing shriek from the challenger.'

The fighters returned to their corners under the cavernous stare of Donna Greeley.

'Well, that was tragic and lopsided,' declared Douglas Bar. 'This oval young man seems to be banking on Trubshaw getting bored looking at his face. I hear tell it is a face remarkably lacking in detail, but he'll develop a few worry lines tonight. If he lives, which now seems unlikely.'

'Thanks, Jim – funny, funny stuff,' Rooster cut in. 'Mind you, there's death and then there's death.'

'True enough, Rooster. Hear about Rohm Crosslin? Tusked by an elephant. That's class.'

'And it's only going to get worse.' Rooster laughed.

In the blue corner, Gregor sat like a mashed potato. The Beast Man was yelling, 'Doesn't courage at least have rarity value in your world?' into his ear when Doctor Perfect, the match medic, stumped up with his knife bag.

'Are you going to introduce me to this mound of jelly which appears to function as a human being?' he asked the Beast Man.

'Never mind all that – patch him up!'

Doctor Perfect leaned over the man on the stool, his permed brain threatening to unravel on to the patient. 'What's up, laddie? Tell the whole dreadful tale.'

Gregor roused a little, tilting. 'Punch,' he slurred, and 'death.'

'Punch death,' the doctor repeated as though enunciating to a simple child. 'My prognosis too, laddie. Manage to snort?'

'Once.'

'Enough to establish your feelings about it, then. Not that it matters. He'll be stepping over your legs before this is over.'

'Don't you have any linament?' shouted the Beast Man.

Perfect flipped a catch and opened his case. 'I have ten paintings of medicine, and a terrible creature which is mainly chin. See?' He removed a strange, furless guinea pig from the case.

'What the hell's that?'

The bell rang. Thrax hustled Gregor to his feet as Doctor Perfect ducked out. Gregor walked into a punch which turned his face to red lace.

'The multi-eared champ ploughs in,' announced Douglas Bar, 'with a series of jabs, hooks and eye-fluttering blandishments which leave the challenger dizzy and slow. The Masked Inconvenience is slobbing around in the corner. He doesn't know or care where he is. Even his stumbling and lolling is far below the standard of a competent boxer. Yet the organisers have been putting it about that this masked man frequently disposes of his opponents in round one. I watched a witch-burning once and the bonfire mother spoke a language to watch – signalling and mouthing to the crowd through the flames as though possessed of new and urgent knowledge. The Masked Inconvenience is making similar motions now to anyone who can bear to look. I'm surprised Trubshaw hasn't knocked him out yet.'

'Knock him out?' Rooster commented. 'That's pushing at an open door, isn't it?'

'The Masked Inconvenience is flailing round and round the outside of the ring, his cries volleying into that crown of ears from many directions and confusing the champ. Now Trubshaw's caught on and belted him to a standstill, and there's a shot under the heart – that punch disturbed his full content, I'm sure. Trubshaw is inflicting a diverse medley of wounds upon his opponent, always advancing. We're seeing a man who doesn't know how to back away.'

'Against a man who doesn't know how to fight,' Rooster chipped in.

'Your evaluation is spot-on, Rooster, though I hate you with the fire of a million suns.'

Gregor yelled and accidentally punched Trubshaw's face as he failed to complete a flinching maneouvre.

'The Masked Inconvenience has scuffed the polished forehead of Trubshaw. It's the first punch he's thrown since this ambush began. Can those inchoate arms encourage Trubshaw to kiss the canvas here today? A body shot has little hope of penetrating that armour. And I thought the omnifurious Trubshaw couldn't get any more upset. Look at him now, pounding the masked man with overhand rights. The challenger is twitching as though hurt at the nerve's core. I heard his skull's ceramic.'

'You just can't help these people, Jim,' said Rooster.

'True enough for our purposes, Rooster. For years to come, these will be the benchmark for terrified screams in the boxing ring. And there's the bell – at which the challenger crawls toward his stool like a first-year drama student.'

The Mayor and the demon Dietrich sat in the shadows. 'It's not very restful, is it?' the Mayor remarked, watching Trubshaw. Between rounds the armoured slob took out his eyeballs, dropping them in grape alcohol solution.

'I suppose you're running a side book on the fight?' Dietrich asked mildly.

'Yes, indeed. Trubshaw's a lock and a lovely boy. He's probably part-mechanical or something.'

'Want to know what I really think, Mayor?'

'If expressed by signs, and uncertain.'

'You're a complete bastard. Well don't look offended – this can hardly be new information. I've seen some horrors since I came here. To discover pedestrians was dismal enough – but you, and this . . .'

'It's an encounter stuffed with combat, that's all. What's the matter with you?'

'You remember that Violaine thing: "The potent theatre of lies and ignorance – this is the value of Parliament." But it's more boring than anything. The fact is, there's a limit, for things like me. I think you need a human.'

Dietrich stood and started walking away sideways along the row.

Mayor Rudloe was spluttering, taken utterly by surprise. 'You'll get yours in hell, Dietrich!'

'I already did, Mayor. But thanks.'

Gregor sat in his corner, all ragged-edged wounds and split meat. He couldn't remember how he'd been roped into this barn dance. His brain had burned out until it was a turkey skeleton with a weak drift of smoke in the cavity. Beast Man Thrax was yelling in his ear, 'The theory of the situation is that you have a mind of your own! That's the theory! And God forgive me for believing it!'

Dr Perfect was prancing gleefully about in front of him saying 'The heart is a terrible loop', or something like that, and waving a bit of hose. Gregor wanted to give him a choice kick in the bollocks and then, why not, he did it. Gregor was so exhausted he didn't stop feeling grouchy when the doctor fell howling. But he knew he'd remember the moment with affection later on.

When the bell rang, Gregor unbent and toppled into the ring, missing Trubshaw altogether and crashing into the carcass of the lady ref. Her neck buckled and the head took a dive in back of the shoulders. Gregor was getting squirly, his senses slow. He saw the head setting like a sun behind the grey torso. Boxing gloves veered across his eyes like inflatable valentines. He was tumbling at Trubshaw, flailing weakly at the tough tortoiseshell skull. A punch landed in the slob demon's face, which squelched like a bath mat. A chorus of recriminations burst from the crowd. Gregor bit into one of Trubshaw's ears, clamping on like a child. No one can blame me for acting like this, he thought with complete assurance. Trubshaw squealed and spun until Gregor was lifted off the ground, attached by the teeth, his legs flying. No one can blame me for acting like this, Gregor thought again, comforted more by the notion than any before. And to think that these were the precise circumstances required to generate it. Life was too specific for generalised wisdom.

The ear came away and Gregor shot into the ropes, tangling there. Trubshaw approached with his right cocked. Gregor received a smack in the mouth – the accident rattled his bones, his gumshield firing upward behind his mask and becoming lodged in his left eye. As he staggered backward he stomped a foot into Donna Greeley's head so that he was wearing it like a boot.

And he saw a phantom in the panels of Trubshaw's armour. It was the image of desire he had pursued into the window of the Ultimatum Restaurant and the Hall of Mirrors – himself. Here was his heaven, his window of escape. Gathering the dregs of his strength, he dived into that pool of loveliness.

Douglas Bar watched as Trubshaw fell like an extinguished fountain. When the slob elected to remain unconscious, Bar slammed words into the mike. 'Trubshaw is down for the count. He looked to be on top in the third until, through a blend of fistic absurdity and happy coincidence, the challenger flew at his gut with both fists. The Masked Inconvenience also knocked out the ref and the match surgeon. Everyone thought we'd be latching his skull to a beam over the local bar, but this twitching lunatic has stirred up a hill of beans. The Masked Inconvenience is the new champ. Though what a reindeer would make of any of this, I don't know.'

'The everyday has bruised all right,' said Rooster. 'You can cook a surprise that big over a slow fire and live off it for a week.'

'The ring is swarming with dissatisfied gamblers. I do declare I'm trying to push through the crowd to get at the new champ for a few simple-minded words. Excuse me, ladies and gentlemen. Here he is – Mr Inconvenience, what was your strategy for the fight?'

'I hoped to allow the ground under me by moving it with these legs, but . . .'

'Dick, get in there and stop it!' Karloff Velocet was heard to shout, at which a silver midget jackflipped over the ropes and tackled Bar by the waist.

In a corner of the chaos, Karloff handed over the Abblatia Angel to Barny, who was chuffed. 'Laugh while you can, monkey boy,' said Karloff. 'I'll see you and your friends at the main presentation. I will hurt your feelings by . . . Look out!'

Gregor's mask had been torn away and he was running from an angry mob, each member of which had quickly committed to breaking a different and distinct bone in his body.

The next edition of *The Blank Stare* would bear the headline FIGHT PROVES USELESS AS ENTERTAINMENT and a subheading OR ANYTHING ELSE.

A picture of Gregor looking shagged out accompanied the caption: 'Mutant blames nobody but himself for pitiful display. Lives in charnel house and is fascinated by pain.'

Ladderland was being stripped down, the clockworks of its decks and gangways exposed. Animals had begun to wander, pestering neighbours with their inscrutable expressions and suddenly clamping jaws. A banished tailor who had wandered back into town was clawed into a bush by Mister Braintree. An old gran glimpsed a spaniel outside her kitchen window, but when she looked again only a vivid smudge of lipstick remained. Gangs of monkeys pounced through town waving useless plastic scissors at disinterested shoppers.

Mister Braintree loped along the beach, strips of gabardine hanging from his mouth. E.H. Hunt admired the lion but pushed his luck, even going so far as to claim that there was such a thing as a 'sea lion'. The sailor now sat on his storage trunk and poked a fire of sea-coral, watching the animal and commenting to the Announcement Horse, 'Continents consort to exile me before my arrival, Nonny. But by God, after a shaky start I was accepted here.' Hunt had tried making a living as a tattoo artist, but he only did pictures of oatmeal and prawns, often on people who did not want a tattoo. He had finally settled into the role of a wily captain who was not believed. He'd shrivelled down like a burger. 'The eyeball is a knot for holding beauty. I've seen a bunch. Dead metals in India, dirty ziggurats in the soaked jungle, deserts of lion-coloured sand.'

'Blindness began underwater,' chimed the rigid Announcement Horse, an ebony totem in ebony sand.

'Here's a riddle for you: I am not mad – nor do I possess reason. I whisk bones and bodies in the chill. A modest cash subsidy will not deter me. I may wear a hat for a short time. I retreat, leaving clammy horrors. What am I?'

'A chef.'

'The sea, you moron, the sea!'

'That again.'

'Listen to the distance, Nonny,' the old captain advised the horse. 'Do you know what piranha music is?'

'Prahna music . . .'

'Piranha. It can only be heard by placing both ears into the water – your whole head, in other words. So nobody has ever returned in a fit state to describe it, a perpetual mystery. What's out there will always be a mystery to you, Nonny, because it's piranha music, all of it. Even if I told you about it, you wouldn't understand – it's something you have to experience for yourself.'

'I weigh one and a half tons,' the horse pronounced without inflection.

Hunt's white-haired leonine head bounced as he chuckled. 'I'll think on the problem. The shore I'll be moving with this boat is not so strong really – land becomes a mere shade.'

'No, the land is strong. It keeps to itself. Do you intend to complete your vessel standing on that half-submerged platform of rock?'

'You have to take your half-submerged platforms of rock where you can at my age.' And Hunt took out a harmonica, tapping the sand out of it to begin playing 'Wedding Veil Jellyfish'.

The lion sat staring out at the ship as its spars and decks grew taller.

10

This Is Yesterday

By the time you've been judged guilty, you've learnt enough about the system to take the moral sting out of it

Barny lifted the hood like a scab and stared at a coalface engine. He hadn't a clue how to rig this car for creeptravel and was glad when the Abblatia Angel showed up, its wings like a couple of white shirts hung in the sun.

'Hello Mike Abblatia,' Barny said. 'This thing needs plugging with muscle junk and etheric shielding. Penny rhino on the dash and spoiler adornments like sovereign rings. Couldn't wake Dot.'

They worked on the valves and servitors until Chloe Low walked by the gas station.

'You see the fight, Chloe?' Barny asked her. 'They were shouting, lashing out, everything.'

'There you go again,' Chloe sighed, walking slowly over the hot forecourt. 'With your animals.'

'Not just that – my house is disappearing.'

Mike Abblatia seemed to fold himself out of the moment, stepping behind the air, then flickered back into solidity.

'The animals are wandering about confused,' Barny continued. 'I'm having to steal the timber back from doomed Eddie Gallo.'

'Have you asked him about it?'

'I suppose I could. "I am searching, I am searching." How does that sound?'

'Like the selfish ravings of a madman. You should think about other people. Why don't you think about how to contribute, Barny?'

'You never used to say so,' said the angel, its voice light as light.

Chloe was about to go when Dugway Thrax the Beast Man wandered by, looking lost and desolate. Barny called him. 'Help us to lift this deathtrap, Mister Beast Man.'

The Beast Man lumbered over and lifted the car one-handed. Barny wheeled a dead mime artist out of the garage on a low trolley, sliding it under the axle. 'Lower away,' he said.

The Beast Man did so, moving against a honey-blond sunset. Chloe was impressed.

Doomed Eddie Gallo was wearing a paper cone on the front of his face when Barny approached him at the canyon edge the next morning. 'What's that on your face, doomed Eddie Gallo?'

'Some sort of paper beak,' whispered doomed Eddie Gallo. 'That funny lawyer gave me the idea, with his harness. You'll have to shout, Barny. One of those sloths went off right next to my eager expression.'

'I wanted to ask you point-blank about this wood!'

'Ah, Barny – I'm finished with wood. But I knew I needed something like wood, in any way at all. And here it is.' He gestured to several hundred packs of rich tea biscuits. 'Bog-standard biscuits of the kind I eat every day. And they will take us to a lovely place perhaps.'

'How will you hold all these biscuits together, doomed Eddie Gallo?'

'Using gull glue,' he said, showing Barny a flattened tube of the stuff. Conceived when King Verbal, attacked by seven doves, stamped on one and noticed that a fluid-like glue emerged from the bird's mouth, gull glue was at first advertised as 'a thinly disguised attempt to bring in democracy by the back door'. When this didn't work, the manufacturers decided to advertise it as 'glue' and sales soared. It was years before Verbal realised he had mis-identified his attackers. 'I've realised the contents of this head of mine are the booby prize in some cerebral lottery,' Gallo continued. 'But I decided long ago that one should live as one's disastrous self, on the grounds of honesty.'

'What if Mayor Rudloe attacks you with a stone?'

'I could use this beak of mine. I might snip a hole in his chin, anything.'

'Will you?'

'Probably not, but you never know. The mood might suddenly overtake me – don't you have unexpected urges like that?'

'I grabbed a fern once when I was walking past, and mashed it.'

'Well . . .' Gallo frowned into the middle distance.

Beltane Carom stood at the centre of his pattern yard, muttering to himself. 'My entire body's a Judas window here. Nothing behind my ribs but pollen. A quick change to one or the other is easy, but both of us at the same time?' He looked about at the mossed frogstands and ferned fountains, and finally at his own shadow before him on the heat-white flagstones. 'So much information stored there. Oh, why not? Fire in the hole.'

He sucked in his breath, and his shadow started to shorten toward him. The light began to flush, reversing its colours. Beltane was shaking as vision wedges opened around him, raking out blood. His shadow was crawling like oil. It retreated beneath him, sucking up through his soles. He darkened, his eyes black.

An air split descended, creasing his brow and proceeding downward. He was dividing like a cell. The process spat off energy which burnt holes in the garden, stirring daygreen sounds from the true mouths of flowers and the moving heads of statuary standing in the soil years. Supporting each other, the two halves of the split began to digress in character, one becoming multicoloured and stupid. Soon a rag and bone jester stood next to Beltane Carom.

Prancer Diego started poncing about like a bastard. 'This violence means more visiting afterwards of churches, to laugh or cry!'

'Shut up!' said Beltane. 'This sudden-death absurdity of yours—'

'Start in panic and there's somewhere to go – begin tired, and we lose. Trumpet that, I reckon!' Prancer wrenched a daffodil from the ground and started playing it like a horn.

The shaman tore the flower from him. 'Karloff demanded we both appear at the ceremony. In matters of ceremony concerning Juno, all patterns must be adhered to. There's probably a reason we don't see yet.'

'Don't spill the pudding on my battleshield Mary!'

'Don't call me Mary. I face you for the first time and—'

'I've a cheese stick for a brain!'

'Damn right you have,' yelled Beltane savagely. 'You'll end up in a cuddle-coat, you bastard.'

'I will die chuckling at something no one else thinks is funny!'

'This rather athletic sarcasm of yours, it's just rubbish and has no place in our . . . get off!'

11

Let's Rock

*Pity the spectators of revolution . . . its success
is not their success, and nor is its failure*

The Mayor entered a circus back yard full of panic artists,
fetches, gut crew and the bustle of preparation. In powder
thick enough to hide a snake, the Fall Marshall stood idly
playing a veda lute among discarded liquorice paper tickets
and drums of goofer fuel. 'Hello, Mayor – you look well.'

'Then the illusion is complete.'

'Cool piglet vest.'

'A bit more austerity would suit this circus of yours.'

'Austerity, you plank? A prefab opulence richer than gold,
that's the stuff. Our second-rate mayhem's lovely, admit it.'

'I refuse to understand you.'

Fang trotted past stretching his perished face. 'Karloff, your
dwarves were meant to wash the previous gore off the
rigging.'

'I can do without the undead getting stroppy, thank you!'

'These meat puppets you glory in,' Rudloe asked the Fall
Marshall as Fang departed, 'all hang and hamstring – what are
they about?'

'Zombies are ideal for acrobatics. They flop about up there
like fish on a line, why not? Circular energy – while I take the
profits. There's beauty.'

'Why did you join the circus?'

'An alibi might as well drip colour.'

'What about family entertainment?'

'The family's finished – it's been replaced by mere relatives.'

A girl pure as snake oil walked past, tattooed around every inch with curlicue cyphers: 'I will organise my faults so that I resemble a public servant' disappeared into her cleavage and emerged 'proud to death' across her belly.

The Mayor was shaking his head in reproach as Cheney scampered over. 'The Vanishing Vorporal has vanished, Karloff.'

'Maybe you should take his name off the posters,' Rudloe suggested.

'Nonsense, he's the most dependable act on the bill,' said Karloff. 'Delivers exactly what he claims, every time. What's the crowd like, Cheney?'

'Alive, for now.' The silver midget strutted away.

The nightmare calliope echoed from the showgrounds. Karloff placed his lute upon a barrel. 'The magic starts in three minutes. The alternative to that arrangement is to release twelve donkeys.'

'Why?' Rudloe asked.

'They're very frightening.'

'Can't you keep your malice under control?'

'Control,' Karloff repeated blankly. 'And where's your demon?'

'A horse in a hoop skirt, eh?' said the Mayor, trying to change the subject as one passed.

'Now,' called Karloff suddenly, 'our masked company are assembled! The day's gaudy extravagances ready for release! Facial stains established! Abandon shrines! Priorities, people – Brian, put a skirt on! Places!'

And he marched past Rudloe, casting the tent flap aside and storming into the big top.

'Perhaps a volcano will erupt,' hoped the Mayor dismally. 'Spewing slag on to the town.'

*

'Why are we here?' Edgy asked as he and Barny took their seats. Dark colours blew through calliope tunes like confetti. 'So I can be ripped open by a bloodthirsty mob again? Those mothers punched me in the belly fifteen times. I counted.' His injuries were a mixed lot. After a day using a hernia for a hammock on Barny's porch and another trying to convince a placid hen it could fly, he felt stiff, his skin like burnt paper over his bones.

'I need you to keep an eye out for Karloff's cheating and betrayal,' Barny told him, looking at the safety net which was suspended above the hippodrome like a giant cobweb. 'Working as a team, we could stab each other awake in front of this rubbish. I can't rely on Gregor now that he's one round bruise. You're my friend.'

'Well, it's true. Oh by the way, me and the Round One are going in together. Those "ceiling toilets" of his are a complete loss. We're opening my beach bar from scratch.'

'What do you mean, from scratch?'

'We're setting up a still by the sea. Sort of stuff turns your face to jelly.'

'Good idea.'

'Thanks. I picked it up in one of those slot machines with the claw.'

Karloff Velocet burst into the round and began grandstanding, shot-voiced and spotlit. 'Karloff Velocet, talky goon and more! I need a second bed for my mouth, that's how smart I am! Wader of sawdust, knot captain of the free, I bring the language of games, dance and artistic performance; all for you, an audience of sleepy cattle! Eruption in each eye guaranteed! You will feel astonishment! We will drive it into you like a nail! There is no escape for you, ultimately!' Briefly the showman blocked his mouth with a rat, then cast it away and proceeded with the announcements. 'We are honoured to perform on Exaction Day – the law taketh away, and the law taketh away. You are the fox doornailed and jerking, his own dreams on his muzzle!'

A bunch of ghoul-clowns exploded into the arena and seemed to be indulging in some sort of all-out tag match – one so dismal as to set half the audience to the activity of idly sketching flowers and birds, which they compared among themselves with raised eyebrows of appraisal.

'Is the Theatre of Misrule a disruptive influence on the universe,' boomed the Fall Marshall. 'Or are we just a small part of it? The clown – emblem of suffering and pain. Nothing gets newer, ladies and gentlemen. Their barely choreographed thuggery makes them the greatest rabble of killers and unhappy madmen ever assembled in one place! They thrive stinking on nasty mysteries and incredulations. Would that I could put a stop to it. Their day-glo irresponsibility sickens me. See them come on like sugar-rot and beware of harmful emissions!'

A clown with cartoon bones tripped on a bucket, breaking his neck.

Karloff used a green glass cane to point out a clown which turned out to have a concave face like the old optical illusion. 'Nothing's the way it seems when it comes to Energy Hog. And "Good grief, what the hell's that?" you may ask. An emu-like bird with a brittle eggshell head – it struts around in a seeming dare to one and all. Crunch me, crunch me! Or do you refer to Boney Panatella, who bears more than a passing resemblance to a wooden spoon? Or Manticore Terry?'

Out pounced a creature with the head of a lion, clawed feet, a barbed scorpion tail and the face of a failure. The Killer Midgets ran around him, trying to ride on his back.

'He's a sawback manticore. Hire a swan if you want – I prefer our Terry. And the Killer Midgets can't keep away – Donald Kagan, Gary Schmitt and Thomas Donnelly there, making his life hell. While Roy Bullock is having such an intricate tantrum you'll have to film it and run the footage at an eighth of the speed to know his concerns. Foon and his Vengeful Autopsy! And notice I'm at great pains to point out the Praline Lad!' A dismay artist manoeuvred his ill-arranged body. 'He has a mango where others have their common sense. Here we observe Tam Sidethroat, long travelled from beyond the soda moat you call death, worked on for ever by a wild pain and decay, bitten by a scary goose, the list goes on. I beg you – have nothing to do with this man. Glaring Ben, the tetchy bear! Lon Horiuchi looks a right charlie as he proves to be a slaughtering psychopath! And here's the Talent Phantom! He will dance for you, not well, but without screaming.'

A man all in black moved tentatively on the sawdust. It was like watching a stone grow. Then he started screaming, as though trapped.

Barny leaned toward Plantin Edge. 'He said he wasn't going to scream.'

'You know how fashions change.'

'Mystifying John Hull – come among us to give something which no one could possibly mistake for a performance!' Karloff sounded vexed, watching John. 'Yes, he has possibilities, and nothing but! And here's Ken the Murky Colossus, and his friend Brad! They've enough indecision to kill a horse. Archer Midland, an archer probably! Mr Patchcoat, who is here to avoid the bother of official investigation! See the sheer wanton damage he can do when challenged! I will repeatedly refer to his activities as "a necessary correction" in order to trivialise the whole matter. Watch!'

Mr Patchcoat pranced round the hippodrome in a shellsuit, foam flying from his mouth as he screamed a paean to relentless hate. Several chimps avoided him, scrambling like living mud over the statue of Violaine and on across the ring to dart among the slow legs of an elephant.

'A necessary correction there, ladies and gentlemen, you'll agree. Perhaps more disturbingly Hatfill Weberman offers us the chance to sublimate our sexual tensions. He can dislocate all his limbs from their sockets!'

'So can I,' Barny hissed to Edgy.

'I think he means Weberman can then put them back again.'

More thoughtful, Barny continued to watch.

'If everything we've been told about him is true, this pickled-onion-flavour savage and self-styled "bouncy bastard" regularly whips himself into a fever. While Ludlow Belcher Belk wishes to be made a part-time member of staff!'

A man ran across the ring pursued by a snorting rhino.

'And this fellow may attack you with a machete! Look out! Hello, Frank! That bastard's a social plague in his own right. Cally the Mess. Sweet, is she? Eight hundred packs of sugar can be a heavy burden! Howe Halabja, playing a waterphone – it's been that kind of a day. Now look above – swapping angles and blocking my vision, yes, it's those demised daredevils, those semi-perished flyers, those liquefaction lads! Approve if you can the putrescent stylings of . . . the Flying Dead Brothers!'

Upon the showboat bar the four revenants waved shredded limbs. 'Buckets of charm!' they choroused and then began the real donkey work of dangling about.

'I'm bored,' Barny whispered to Plantin Edge, who nodded. They wandered outside and the circus seemed a world away, the concession stands mostly abandoned. Wandering west toward the Furfur district, they passed through some deal trees and entered the scrub around the pennyground.

Edgy kicked at dry cortex cacti. 'What are your thoughts, Barny?'

Barny knelt on the ground, tilling over fluff and feathers snarled up with stones. 'I wonder if I do the right things. Chloe makes me wonder.'

'She's just trying to get at you. Now that you've split up she'll travel miles to pump poison gasses into your mental atmosphere.'

'I don't care. I could use those gasses. Look at me, I'm a nervous wreck.'

'Well,' said Edgy uncertainly, scrutinising his placid friend, 'maybe you could vent your lusts with some o' them magazines you turn sideways.'

'*Snake Keeper's Weekly*?'

'You and your critters. I hear Mister Braintree's been scudding about, nipping the legs of one and all.'

'Yeah, I hear he got a tailor who dared come back into town.' Barny related how the man's yells provoked the laughter of passers-by. The tailor had begged a Gubba Man for help and the silent sentry held him in place while the lion dined upon his ravelled innards. If you've ever meddled with a four-hundred-pound cat, you'll know this is the last thing you need. 'Meanwhile my house is being gradually stolen – the winged and stepping animals of the earth have only half a home to go back to.'

Edgy suggested that they walk back to town for the animal presentation ceremony. 'Those tigers are probably creaming themselves in anticipation.'

Meanwhile in the top, Karloff gestured up at the zooming cadaverines. 'The Flying Dead Brothers there, real card-carrying revenants, leaving one and all bewildered and probably damned. And now, to interrupt your enjoyment of the meat and potatoes of the show, your own Mayor appears upon his expensive balcony above.'

In the bowed mouth of Rudloe Manor's balcony, the Mayor was lying half-in half-out of a cannon barrel. He could see the hippodrome and the central showground through the high web of the safety net. With a numb, hammy hand he wiped his brow. A chalky corpse swung by at eye level.

'The Mayor is unteachable. His brain seems to be a ball of tinfoil. My words vibrate it merely. He is not equipped to solve the sad mystery of his appointment to office. Even his attempts to stifle innovation have failed. Now he has contracted to fire himself from a cannon. A foolhardy stunt, Mayor. You were mad to suggest it.'

'Me?' squawked Rudloe, and was shoved into darkness by a sudden clown with a plush head and a gob like a rubber rainbow.

'Delicious concrete awaits you, m'Lord. As your local philosopher once said, "I have never seen a scorpion shrug – I have never seen a government err to the good. I've seen monsters being born in newsprint. Corruption is only self-vanquished – thus corruption is not vanquished. I am certain of nothing but trouble." I hope you're wearing your flame-retardant underwear. Dynamite doesn't mess around.'

Filling with nausea, Rudloe felt a surge of black heat as reversed-acid colours sucked toward him.

He smashed faultlessly through the swinging zombies and caused one of Fang's legs to boomerang into the screaming audience.

Then he was snagged in the safety net amid assorted rotten limbs. Karloff was dancing by below him. The audience's response to his splashdown, if any less impassioned, would have been undetectable.

Then a roar went up. At first Rudloe assumed it was his dismal electorate's usual delayed reaction. But the shout was one of alarm. As he twisted about, Rudloe saw a massive black construction toiling and barging toward him. 'Stein-way!' he screamed, struggling.

'Merriment concluding!' Karloff cried. 'Piano joy beginning!'

'So Max was right. You've been keeping these black-lacquered bastards for your own ends.'

'Never fear,' the Fall Marshall assured him in a confidential tone. 'That tragic creature works by a series of reducing gear ratios.' Then he raised his voice for the audience. 'In the spirit of fair play I just told him he was safe, but in truth this net's purpose is anything but safety. Would it surprise you, Mayor, to hear the safety net's made of nerves?'

'Nerves? You usually use a few old veins.'

'True, but these nerves are all the better to alert the Steinway spiders to the presence of prey.'

Hearing the plural, Rudloe wrenched around to see a second piano surging forward from the other direction. The crowd began to panic, climbing over each other to get out of the tent.

'Metal springs – man's oldest foe! And their turning arc's a killer, I'm afraid. You may run but you cannot escape the ebony racket of these legendary automata – Sterling and Dragbelly!'

The nearest Steinway slammed its lid on the zombie Ladaat, scarfing him back with discordant chimes and then continuing toward Rudloe, pistoning its eight black enamel legs.

'Isn't there a danger someone could get hurt?' someone stopped to posit from the fleeing audience, and was shoved aside by citizens galore.

'I wish pleasures were quieter,' another commented, and was punched to the floor.

Rudloe watched the populace run. Whimpering his weight, a scream of retreat was his only strength. 'Help! I'm a rookie at this sort of thing!'

Sterling fiddled massively closer, the heavy contraption bowing a deep dent in the net. Fang's head rolled downhill.

It was these dull circumstances which conspired to free me from my earthly tether. As I once said, 'It's an illusion to believe you're not ruled, unless you do what you're forbidden to do.'

Something was wobbling through the sky like a bat. Was one of the Brothers still aloft? The object was joined by another and they swooped in a flash of thin-skinned wings. The two defector demons Dietrich and Gettysburg, scabbed with scales and silver with blades, blurred above the crowds and phased in and out of the local bandwidth. Dietrich seemed to be eating a chocolate egg and Getty was wearing some sort of car coat. It was as if they had dropped by casually between other activities.

Veins showed in the back-illuminated wings as they descended upon Sterling. The Mayor's eager, upturned face didn't change at all as they clamped on to the piano and hauled the machine aloft, beating hard. Loose hammers chimed at the wires as they lifted it across. Its black legs were clawing at air. Then the Steinway fell from their grasp and slammed upon the Violaine statue like a judge's gavel upon the rights of man.

My monument shattered like plaster as the other Steinway fled the scene and the safety net collapsed. The etheric leash unravelled and I bloomed out invisible, free as disease. Air surrounded kleig lights which swept past my escape – I blurred over this vale of entrances and tropic-slow angels stirring like heat. Momentary people stood undoing bundles of air. They were already perfection, merely folded and complicated into disguise. By virtue of being a ghost on the way out, I was feeling soft. Here were wide pathless times and simple breath. I slowed to look back on curiosity, nothing left now but to watch the end. No longer hooked upon the sky, I slipped between gaps in the colour with a victim's success. Me, you bastards – Bingo Violaine.

12

He do the Police in Different Voices

Language will die of slow starvation

The troops normally refused camouflage because it bored them to tears, but today they tried some of that bark-effect stuff the Sarge had told them the frogs wore. Within minutes of donning the things they had forgotten about its glories. A Steinway piano was amok in the Coum district and when they arrived, Dragbelly popped and clattered, whipping strings at prim madams and necklacing blood over pale faces – all inside of a minute. A Gubba Man was smashed aside and burst open against a street lamp, a body without organs.

The Sarge gestured the entire length of the suburbs. 'Terminate these lights. I'll watch.'

'It's done, Sarge,' Perkins said, presenting the illustrated *Four Sky Code* with a shy glee.

'Done, Perkins?' the Sarge rumbled. 'We'll see.' And he frowned down at the translation with a judicious eye. Then his large face brightened. 'Good work, Gibbs. A bit blocky but you've caught the subtleties. And these birds, Perkins – beautiful.'

'It'll help tame and impound this leggy bastard,' shouted Gibbs, pointing at the specialty behemoth.

'Be rational, boy. And by "rational" I mean the condition which will exist when we're finished here and have all calmed down.'

Up the driveway the piano dragged its stomach, its lid slamming open and closed with a sheen like black glass. The Sarge glimpsed sinews of octavial wires as he approached. 'Resistance harvests excitement from the dynamic tension, lads,' he said. 'And it builds up the balls.'

'Really, Sarge?'

'That's right, Ripper.' The Sarge vaulted over the creature's legs and hit the flatbed of its back. 'Tilted marvels viewed on the level, they are marvels still.'

The hulking beast began to balk.

Waste messes up your life, the Sarge was thinking, quite placidly. *Action. Remember it. Remember.*

More troops scurried up and put the boot in as the Sarge continued to rodeo. 'I attack,' said Gibbs. 'Barracks twinkle with apprehension.'

This retinue of jellyheads could be strangled by joined-up writing, thought the Sarge in the calm oasis of his head. *But a statement can be a set of triangulation coordinates. It won't necessarily make sense where you are – it points to the place where it'll line up perfect and ring like a bell. Those places are usually quite interesting. Of course, this is a luxury and of no use if you're hungry or in danger. Yes, I'm really a fortunate man.*

And suddenly the beast went still beneath him, all becalmed. The lads stepped back as their leader climbed down from the creature's back and drew up an empty crate, sitting before the keyboard. The spider sat low as though dead and dry, its legs clawed in underneath. 'Here we go, Gibbs,' said the Sarge, and began to play, singing the difficult translation of *Four Sky Code*:

> *every time we stride*
> *our many legs collide*
> *look to science*
> *to exterminate us and our kind*

oh, the shadow of a bird
is softer than a bird
but stroke the shadow
and be bitten by a snake.
Three hundred puppets with one voice!
There's an endorsement

and fear may stop for breath
but I'll continue biting your face
for I am the law
clamping hard to my wages.
You will solve all my problems.

oh, the eye of a dog
is made of dog
but touch the eye
and be bitten by a dog.
Three hundred puppets with one voice!
I must claim they are different

my face is too close
for you to remain undiseased.
You will solve my dilemma.
Take this terrible duty from me
I will pay you a small stipend.

oh, the face of a cow
is smaller than a cow
but stroke the face
and be bitten by a cow.
Three hundred puppets with one voice!
Report it as their victory

'Oh yes,' he said, concluding with relish. 'Heaven grills a ladybug – top of the summer!'

'We love you, Sarge. Hooray for the Sarge, a geezer!'

Under a sickly, forensic sky, riggers were already striking the big tent. A ramped stage had been set up before the frontage of Rudloe Manor. Barny and the Mayor stood upon it, crowded by some stinking orchid arrangements. The populace, tempted by the false promise of 'dogs with merry eyes and ears of velvet, and the quiet and privacy to enjoy such charms', was already growing suspicious and restless. Beltane Carom had a venomous yellow headache. It had been exhausting, sucking up the shadow where the other man was stored, and then the split. Now both Beltane and Prancer stood drained and quavery, spectating from opposite sides of the stage. Neither cast a shadow.

Karloff mounted the stage in a cloth-of-gold robe and arcane cuffs for effect. His wraparound hat revolved ever upward. Rudloe immediately snapped at him, 'You've got some explaining to do!'

'How do you feel?' asked Karloff, bland and affable.

'Like a fried maggot, if you must know. The worse for having to contain m'sizzling rage.'

'Why are you in a bad temper, Nelly?'

'Your diverse cavorts and bagatelles damn near ripped my head off! And don't call me Nelly!'

'You wouldn't even begin to understand the real reason why we do these things. But even you knew it was an imprudent challenge.'

'Imprudent? It was hell! Everyone here saw it and some were taking detailed notes!'

'Carnival critics. Their praise has paralysed my work. But I suppose you call that democracy.'

'Democracy is the whisper of a near-dead clown trapped beneath a street grating, heard for one uncertain second and dismissed as a laughable irrelevance.'

'Can I quote you on that?'

'You bloody crook. You'll understand the sky between bars.'

'Shall we get on with this ridiculous ceremony?'

'Yes!' the Mayor agreed bitterly.

But before they could get started they had to watch a display of Rooster's hydraulic pants – these he inflated with an industrial-strength bellows and feed-pipe which he attached to his dungarees. Both Rudloe and Karloff became increasingly impatient, and Rooster himself was clearly baffled. He gave a running commentary during the demonstration, the last few minutes of which was inaudible. Though the audible parts were rammed with contradictions and vagueries, most of the onlookers were too drunk to consider it a bad omen.

The Mayor bellied forward before he had decided which expression to wear, and the result was a sort of sweaty blank. 'Rooster there, going straight to the heart of things as usual. Farewell Rooster, you back out dressed brutally. Well, we've endured some corny routines over the last few days, and some of us have come to grief. I thank the Circus of the Heart's Shell for providing the public with another distracting consolation. Later on today, you will salute the needs of your leaders. And just as we provide a tent for your subsequent recovery, relationships too must be healed, which is what this ceremony is about. You all know about the feud between Barny Juno here and the Fall Marshall, regarding the freedom of the winged and stepping animals of the earth, most of them quite lethal. The signs are that they have reached an agreement. Karloff Velocet will address you now, with his stark malevolence.'

'Thank you, Mayor. Given the limitations of this wrecked parish our travelling company have provided you all a fine entertainment, if a little bit chancy.'

Ninety eyes locked closed against the speaker's bragging.

'Consider, I beg of you – you failures who thrive in this hotbed of lethargy and torpor – the mirths and upheavals we have shown you. The clown, his acrylic gob bending glumly downward. The spitter of fire and his threatening behaviour, his implied demand that you be impressed. The dead man drooping from bits of string. Those heroes have to live by clear practical rules, not by blear generalisations like you bastards. Or like Mayor Rudloe, who apparently feels he can zoom out of a cannon without any special effort.'

Rudloe butted in with a forced smile. 'I believed him in the crowd – I mistrusted him when his features advanced.'

'Your Mayor,' Karloff continued, waving what seemed to be a piece of rubbery ham for emphasis, 'having loused it up in grand style, blames me for his recent failure. Our contradictions annoy the tidy-minded. From worm one we have been ominous and said as much. We are the golden shame. Nothing must be left to chance.'

Behind Karloff, Barny tried to spot Chloe in the crowd. There was just the dog Help and a mass of folk standing idle. Edgy was there too, dressed in a sheet – he never missed a chance to see the Mayor talking gibberish. A few clowns were leading the Fatal Rhino up the ramp toward the podium.

On opposite sides of the stage, both Beltane Carom and Prancer Diego were shaking, the air around them fluttering with instability. Beltane realised the separation was feebly anchored. He couldn't keep it down. He and Prancer started to distort weirdly toward the stage, blots of flame flaring behind their teeth.

'I concede defeat,' Karloff was reciting, 'and honour my agreement with the halfwit Juno. My animals are his, and by ceremonially snogging the Fatal Rhino, he inherits ownership of them all. I have enjoyed inconveniencing you with my antics. I have often been called an idealist. In fact I am a killer and a criminal. As Violaine said, "muscle across rooms, through leagues of rage, veins full of grey wind, 'til murder is reached". Greatness is all.' He threw down the Moral Fibre with studied nonchalance, believing that the crowd knew and cared what it was. 'And many die as greatness's lesser, fading echo.'

As Barny stepped forward to snog the rhino, Karloff pulled

the Wesley Kern gun from under his golden robe and swept it at him.

On either side of the stage, Beltane and Prancer were stretching and multiplying toward each other like soap bubbles – two distorting images trying to merge.

'From Sweeney,' Karloff said, finding the trigger. 'And from me.' Then a fleshy conflagration flooded in at him from two directions, trapping him like a bug in gum. Karloff's hat exploded, scattering glass and some brain matter over the assembly. The air was tainted with a plasma spritz and the stench of ozone. He was a standing, moaning mass of limbs and merged faces, his own stirred in with that of Beltane and Prancer. Two spines were visible, twisted around each other like a giant DNA strand. The Wesley Kern gun was pushed through the arrangement like a sausage stick.

Beltane was alarmed. 'Flypaper!'

'Trapped like kings!' Prancer cried, laughing.

'Who'll protect Juno?'

The Karloff face was screaming. Barny stood by in mild confusion. The audience was surprised enough to applaud.

'Well,' Rudloe told them, hiding his slight bewilderment, 'that concludes the ceremony. Pick up any rubbish as you leave, please.'

Barny gave the rhino a quick peck on the cheek as Help skittered up and ate the Moral Fibre.

Like a funeral reversed in the sun's saturation, a curlicued and feathered procession tumbled through town with Barny at its head. Here was the simpleton whose garden was home to eight hundred eels, who flew upon a swan, whose trousers were alchemised to fallen trousers as he spoke words of sorcery, now proving tidiness an absurd and unnecessary myth. His core audience of affronted bastards found their eyes pinned open by a sort of vivid delirium of forms. A tiger the size of a car, a rhino like a tusken boulder, an elephant like walking drought earth, a panther as sleek as a seal and black as a beetle, a crocodile with teeth the size of Brazil nuts, cowprint zebras and paper-headed birds like rod-puppets, a living tumble of fur and biology. Crowded species were flowing together, mates and foes mixed as though crayoned by a kid, wed in tooth and claw like saints beyond nameable colour.

Outnumbered by undulating detail, Barny drew to a halt at the gate to his house. Nothing remained but the gate, some rubble and a burst sofa on which Gregor lay, bruised and bandaged and covered in leeches.

Barny's bland countenance drained out. 'Is this all there is?' he said. 'Gregor?'

'Except these slugs . . . oh, my lovers!'

'Gregor, what's the *matter* with you – slugs?'

'They applied themselves to my wounds and now I adore them.'

'Oh,' Barny said, already distracted. He was wax-pale against the golden coats of new lions.

'Bubba?' Gregor was calling as Barny wandered away.

The animals, not knowing where to go, gathered amiably around the couch, where Gregor was sitting up in gradual anxiety.

13

Roll Away the Stone

Lucifer is a black glove we wear to hide our own fingerprints

Hearing about the public appearance of the Wesley Kern gun, Chloe Low went to ask Karloff about it. What she found at the centre of the circus turmoil was a clumsy, tilting amalgam of Beltane Carom, Prancer Diego and the ringmaster. 'We're upping sticks, missy. Clearing out. Karloff's idea – my idea. It's his idea, Miss Low, he's got stuff to hide. Rather ironic, really. Then some meat was eaten by Help and fell under his fatal spell. Our flesh and blood is in debt to Mother. Shut up, Prancer.'

'What happened to *you*, Beltane?'

'Me and Prancer couldn't stay divided long and good old Karloff here got in the middle. He was about to shoot Barny and everyone else, as far as we could tell. As many people as I could, anyway.' This last was added by Karloff himself, his head melded with that of Prancer. At the joining point was an eye with a twin pupil like a black double egg. 'Life is never the whole story. We're sorry we can't give you back the gun but as you see . . .' The triple man gestured to the rigidly impaled rifle.

The carriages of the loco vimana had been re-coupled and loading was almost complete. A withered clown stumbled over holding a wooden frame stretched with skin. Stitched into the centre of this contraption were some bone fragments and teeth.

'Is Barny all right?' Chloe asked.

'He went off with the animals,' said Karloff, and wheeled the whole body about to view the exit frame. 'That'll do. Put it over there. All aboard!' Beltane turned the body to Chloe. 'Goodbye, Miss Low. You'll have to take care of your Juno now, if you can. Most pupils teach the same thing back, eager to please, but not him. In this age, an honest man is like a grenade thrown into a crowd.'

Fang took a last look and boarded the creep train with his brothers. Clowns, tumblers, huxters and hoosiers leapt aboard, including several local mimes desperate to escape persecution. These were shoved out as Karloff-Beltane-Prancer stepped up to the head engine and activated the massive rack of spectral palladium valves. The train shunted off with the pale stares of geeks at the windows, accelerating toward Grapefruit Integrity Swoon Street and the framed fragments of Rod Jayrod's head. The hull of black and gold was already blurring as the engine hit the exit frame and the scarship streamed behind a hole in the air, disappearing in a blast of goofer exhaust.

Chloe went to Barny's house and found only a dusty lot, a smashed sofa and the bug-eyed Golden Sid sort of casting about amid the trash in bent spectacles, his gob a howling hole already emptied of sense. Sid had worked for Barny for years taking care of the animals and now seemed lost. He pointed to the southwest, sobbing.

'This car is some sort of passenger thing.'

'That's what I've been telling you, doomed Eddie Gallo.'

'Those head-swords of yours are dripping vinegar everywhere.'

'Pay attention, doomed Eddie Gallo. Unclip the jump cables. *God* almighty!' Inside Gaffer's steepled head was a mind like a dead tooth. He tried to rub some vitality into the emptiness as doomed Eddie Gallo stood vacantly with the jump clips hanging from his hand like dead snakes.

The muscle car they were fussing around in the garage bay was painted fire-apple red and had a hood ornament like a syringe. Max Gaffer was already in the driver's seat when the Abblatia Angel appeared in the inner office doorway, its half-open wings skimming the frame. 'Every forty minutes I shock it off a stainless steel doughnut coil.'

'Eh?' Gaffer snapped, taken by surprise. 'Er, well why?'

'It would seem appropriate that I do so.'

'Appropriate.' Gaffer chuckled, relaxing a little at the angel's ineffectiveness. 'There's what you get from dying on a budget, eh, doomed Eddie Gallo?'

Gallo waved amiably at the angel. 'Hello Mike Abblatia.'

'Hello doomed Eddie Gallo. An artist pulls love from chaos.'

'I hear you, my friend. Max Gaffer here is full of ideas.'

'Get in the car, doomed Eddie Gallo,' the demon lawyer told him, leaning under the dash and sparking the hot-veins.

'Right-o,' said Gallo, getting into the passenger seat all jolly as the engine fired up.

'Are you stealing this vehicle, then?' asked the angel calmly.

'It's not all bottled endings and laughter, Abblatia,' shouted Max Gaffer above the roar. 'That's a pigment of your imagination. Go to hell.' And whooping, he swerved the car across the forecourt and into the street, driving away.

Gaffer steered with one hand and raised a megaphone with the other blaring, 'Doomed Eddie Gallo. His philosophy is reputed to have marvellously restorative powers when ignored. Get down honkies.' He turned to Gallo without lowering the megaphone and blasted, 'That'll hook those bastards and their rotted-out principles.' Sticking his head out the window, he told the town that 'Gallo will now jump the canyon in the most daring venture to oh I can't be bothered.' He threw the hailer aside as they arrived at the fragile ramp of rich tea biscuits.

The only onlookers were two children – one made of tin, one made of gilled meat. 'I got my invite,' Maquette called, waving.

Gaffer, becoming only vaguely aware that some of the gears were off at odd angles, backed up a way, lining up on the ramp. They sat there, the engine turning over. 'Well, doomed Eddie Gallo?'

Gaffer was feeling the floor. 'This picture carpet is full of ink. Shall we go, Gallo?'

Gallo looked ahead at the twisted ramp. 'It's what I've worked towards, I suppose. All right. Push the button, Max.'

With the hum of servitors and meat valves firing, the view accelerated into stretched geography. The car surged forward, dragged lightning behind it.

As the kids watched, it balked on to the ramp, rocketed above the abyss, convulsed and disappeared in midair.

The car was bouncing through billowing twists of pain and cold entropy, an icily transparent universe of sickly nerves. The vehicle they had stolen was clearly a scarcar with pig-trotter indicators and a baffler stuffed with discredited passes. They were firing down the etheric creep lanes, flashing past dead dimensional port authorities of necrotic grey. White razorbahns tumbled toward the windshield and fluxions beat the panelling. Swelling into view ahead and to the right was Karloff's vimana train, the hull's gold running to liquid.

'I didn't bring any biscuits,' said doomed Eddie Gallo.

'What?' shouted the lawyer, his form a silhouette as fizzing incineration lashed past the window. He had never been this far out before. 'Are you aware of our situation, doomed Eddie Gallo?'

The shrinking locomotive powered out of their lane's bandwidth, venting goofer fuel and sending a chilling wallop through their skulls. They began to fluoresce. Barbed ropes glowed amid them. These were delirium organs, ghostly until required, exclusively toxic. Now they glittered into solidity, corrosive absence gone rampant. 'Er, wait a minute for really strident strategy yelling,' Rudloe cautioned the blurring labyrinth, holding up a momentary hand and clearing his throat. Then he hollered 'Help me!', his mouth tromboning like an old cartoon. Shrivelled highways clobbered up over the hood, exploding both windshields.

'It's too late for all that,' snapped the lawyer, blue ice flames tearing across his metal faceplate. Max Gaffer had taken his bearings by a constellation of crappy ideas and now rushed pell-mell to a bog-standard doom. 'Sorry, Gallo,' he said, and his head blew apart, scattering through the empty rear windshield.

Gallo looked aside at the headless driver. Part of the smile bridle hung on, flapping like a tow bar.

The vehicle was calming a little, the channel walls becoming visible. Doomed Eddie Gallo saw nested bones, demons up on blocks and the hanging threads of civilisation, then the car coughed into open space, dirty oxygen flying beside the door. With a jarring smash, the car was scudding to a halt in a slash of white dust.

Shaken, doomed Eddie Gallo climbed out of the scarcar into a wasteland of dry riverbed diagrams. Golf balls and pebbles cracked in the desert. A parched feral scream cut through the poison air from nearby. It was the sound of bandages over bones, a shelled species of raw survival.

On some scrubby desolation a little way east of the boneseed factory, the blood shed was doing strong business. It was a corrugated structure covered in pepperbird droppings and painted-over Cyrillist slogans. Only a metal chimney against a bush suggested that anything lay underground.

The Mayor passed the line of citizens who were queuing to give, ignored the levy pumps and slipped through a hidden door, entering the antique elevator. Underground, he walked down the silverine hallway and entered the chamber of the Conglomerate. The intake pumps were jumping with each pulse of fluid, feeding the flushed biomass which filled the room. 'Ah, extraction day. It's a very good year, Mayor.' Several other voices agreed, chuckling glutinously.

'I want to penalise the Church of Automata for hiring out those mechanical spiders.'

'The Church of Automata? A production line built from human bones? I doubt they'll feel much abashed. And the community's always seen the spiders as an outside threat. Distraction's good for them and good for us. Not one brown penny will be spent on their long-term happiness.'

'Events themselves sit on the fence,' said another mouth amid the bulging biology. 'We need an occasional occasion. Don't you think?'

'Yes, yes, no, you're right, yes. What about Karloff?'

'Recent evil is fickle. Evil grown from infant depths has a stronger foundation. How did you react to his antics?'

'I cared steadily, my reaction arranged beforehand.'

Rudloe glanced around at the palpitating walls and perspiring pipes. Everything was stained red.

'And did you enjoy the show, Mayor?'

Rudloe laughed uneasily. 'I'm not a common citizen.'

'Your duty – as a citizen – is to help us pretend we're not the bad guys. That you are not taxed under threat. That all are created equal. That our office is earned. That there is no luck or privilege. That there is justice. And this you have done as an example to all.'

'I may yet tell all,' said Rudloe quietly.

'Oh dear,' gurgled another voice. 'He was doing so well.'

'I will,' said Rudloe, attempting truculence. 'I'll walk over there like nothing you've ever seen, and tell them where the blood goes.'

'See what it changes, when you tell the truth to cowards. We've been gnawing the meat from the floating rib of this province for years. Today, if I'm not mistaken, you flicked away your last vestige of dignity like a bit of rolled snot. You are ready to join us.'

The Mayor sensed a trap. 'Join you?'

'Now, now, don't thank us – you've earned it.'

The Mayor stared at the steaming elite in stricken silence. Faced with the prospect of being incorporated into a multi-slob of farting blebs and stinking ligaments, his mind's grasp was slippery. The translucent wall of a large stomach displayed a slosh of red liquid. The Conglomerate always joked about 'transparent government' – here it was. The pumps were hammering.

'Advance, Rudloe,' the voices chorused, and one added: 'Let's meet in the morgue and pull out all the stops. Whatya say?'

'You're raving.' Rudloe's voice trembled.

'Grow up, Mayor – leave deniability behind. Know the truth, freeing the relief and tragedy at once.'

Rudloe took a step forward. 'Is a thing freed by knowing it?'

'It helps one's strategy to know the truth of a situation. Gallo or someone can take over, so long as the machinery's the same. He's a useful idiot, a fully paid-up moron. Even by the smart an accurate conclusion may always be adroitly avoided.'

Rudloe slipped in gore, yelping. He lunged for a handhold, his arm plunging into jellied meat. Then he felt it being sucked in solid until he was up to the elbow. His face began to push into the flubbering guts. 'You're nothing but gall and greed!' he blurted in a rush of candour, just before his mouth filled with blood and transparent fat.

'Keep telling yourself that, Mayor. Structure is imposed. There is no centre – it needn't hold. We make our own centre. We take.'

Rudloe lay suspended in the slicks, veins threading through him, sumps bypassing his alimentary system. He screamed into meat.

*

Maybe Chloe was right, Barny had thought. He should do some of these things that people seemed to want, that normal people took for granted. He would do his social duty and then drop by the recovery tent.

He felt strange as he waited in line. There didn't seem to be any animals around here; no birds sang. Hammering machinery sounded from the metal shed. Barny noticed that B.B. Henrietta was in line in front of him. 'Hello, B.B.'

'Barny. I heard you stood up in the town square and shrieked racial abuse till the cows came home.'

'Did I?'

'Yes.'

'Oh.'

'Not a good idea, Boo. You'll find that strangers, up close, become more craggy, but remain strangers.'

Pale, shaky people wandered out and past them. The line shuffled forwards and he and B.B. were inside.

'Best avoided then? Strangers?'

'Yes.' She saw a cubicle vacate and grimaced nervously. 'Oh, this is me. See you later.' She went into a pump booth and closed the door.

Barny felt lonely. He found himself wishing Mr Low, Chloe's father, were here to talk to.

A booth was vacated and Barny went over, feeling strange. He closed the door behind him and lay back on the oblique-angled surgical table. Relationships too must be healed, he remembered from somewhere. A glass ribcage closed upon him, two racks of spikes piercing his body. Barny was surprised at how much it hurt. The glass turned dark red as blood began to exit. Barny was seeing warm smoke moving through his head. He thought of the hot fur of bears in the sun. He was feeling unfocused, couldn't pin any information down. It was like his mind had disappeared, leaving his closed eyes and a body. He wandered over the thought of his animals, Help's lipsticked face, Gregor resting finally on the lion's head and the leopard raking open Edgy's face at a jaunty angle. Edgy laughing fit to burst, Dumbar's placental head, Fang snogging bat after bat in the sorting office, Beltane Carom in his garden, a current of slow liquid flowing from one to the other of his raised hands. Mister Braintree yawning like an adder. Maquette and Spooky Staring Child among the dreamspores and activans of the Shop. The Mayor, growing redder and fatter than the town. Mr Low, he could see him clearly – an old man pure as old water, his corrugated forehead, the stitching of wrinkles around his eyes, teeth like sunflower seeds and a parchment voice. 'A riot of nature is the definition of a riot.' Chloe's perfectly pale face moving with a smile. Everything moved slowly, strange tastes staining space, clouds fighting over the sky, fogs rolling the land in darkness, numbness among nothing else.

Barny's own face was sucking in, ageing as tissues imploded. No over-levy warning sounded, because it never did. Only a clean-up crew was alerted.

A vermilion rain was falling in the gutty cellar. The huge coral abdomen heaved. Rudloe's thick tongue caught ruby drips from above and retracted into the mass. 'So regret me.'

'What, you don't like it?'

'No, I like it, I like it . . .'

'There are no secrets between us any more, I hope.'

'How can there be?' laughed Rudloe, a smear in the bloodshot anatomy. 'And why do the work of hiding? That's the point.'

'The point,' jabbered the other voices, echoing in a flurry of corpuscles. 'He has one, after all.'

'That a lie will find itself surrounded by competition. Maybe that's not the business to be in. Point taken.'

A ripple passed through the Conglomerate, rubbery guts flubbering. It reared, weak veils of pink membrane tearing. The mass stretched toward the north wall and surged through the entrance to the ancient pipe which long ago donated a minuscule token of the levy to the blood clock.

Dry dirt spuffed up in a trail passing Spacey's Gas Station, Del's Fright Foundry and a goat waiting for a taxi. The Conglomerate passed under the town square and ascended into Rudloe Manor, infecting the architecture and blotting every room with a shrieking hurricane of blood. Pouring down the pipes and gutters of the blood clock, the crimson committee burst from the eaves, clotting across the palace facade like knotty red gargoyles. A dozen sticky meat faces stretched and mouthed from the stonework. 'Why hide? Let our citizens do the pretending. It's what they want.'

Chloe met Edgy in Butane Reply Street. He was pushing a cart bearing Gregor and a metal keg. 'Hello Chloe,' said Edgy. 'Can you spot the relief in my face? I've given up on society at last and am pushing Gregor around in a cart.'

'Where's Barny?'

'He left Gregor surrounded by woolly monsters. Gregor ran as fast as his arms and legs could take him. Baying pursuers have always been the key to staying slim.'

'Except in my case,' Gregor said. 'I weigh more and believe less.'

'Your final state may be that of a dead whale,' Chloe observed.

'I'd like that.'

'Which way did Barny go?'

'He went all embryo on me. Followed the crowd toward the Blood Shed. Maybe he was going to pay.'

Chloe followed the violet grey of the sky toward the milking shed. When she reached the building the line had been exhausted. Only a couple of cubicles were occupied, and these occupants wilted out, leaving the building and heading for the recovery tent. Going outside into strange silence, Chloe stumbled across broken black tarmac hairy with weeds. She circled the tin building. Overgrown behind the shed lay broken bricks, rotten car tyres and dead sump equipment.

Two or three dry husks also lay here, like bundles of dark red sticks. These were levy skeletons, lives discarded in favour of the mechanism. Conceding to what was expected, Barny had died out of hand.

14

The Vigil (The Sea)

Justice knows when it's not wanted

'Barny says you want a job here.' B.B. Henrietta nodded darkly. She bumped four closets closed and started pointing out features of interest in the dungeonlike basement of the sorting office. She gestured to the sweating walls. 'These barnacles – don't be tempted to prise them off the walls, they've been here for years and the meat is way tough and tastes bitter. That bracket fungus over there has a mouth containing a set of gnashers, you can feed it raisins if you like.' Flipping a hand at some black bats in the eaves, she gave a withering look. 'Those are wall-warmers, smacker-bats. To keep you from getting lonely, if you know what I mean. The thermostat is a marshmallow, that should give you an idea of the way we do things down here. Oh these dangling soft bladders are just for show.' She pointed at Dumbar, who sat in a dim corner, his placental head sagging aside. 'Mister Airbag Head over there – his head's full of rain, so what? Aren't you even remotely interested in the particulars of the job?'

'Yes, I am,' the Beast Man assured her quickly.

'Stuff comes down the delivery chute on to the long sorting table here. You take a hold of the stuff, and depending on the size and shape, get rid of it one way or another. If you don't know what to do, if you're not sure about anything, say,

"Lizards crowd the censor." That's code for us to start ignoring you, or keep ignoring you if we are already. Say it enough and you may not even get paid. Our boss is the Captain. Bloody cheek treating us with such understanding. Enthusiasm's at a premium round here. Think coldly about this place and all your memories, and you'll be respectable enough.'

Dugway Thrax looked at the watercooler. Three pale scorpions scuttled at the bottom of the tank. 'How do we get rid of the . . . "stuff"?'

'Oh, burn it, eat it, drive it over a cliff in a dodgy Anglia, whatever you can think of, really. The best way is the Drop over here – a sort of vacuum vortex.' She pointed at a large open corner of pinwheeling darkness. 'Sometimes you need to soften stuff up before you chuck it in there. And this is Gregor's oven, from when he used to work here. Around noon the boiler flames red.'

'Does that matter?'

'Not really. Trip on the secret slices if you want to fall. Sorry if I'm going over stuff you already know or what's obvious.'

'Thanks, Miss Henrietta,' Thrax said with a shapeless apprehension.

Several boxes and bundles pushed through some bacon hangings and slid down the delivery chute, barging on to the sorting table. 'Grab the big one!' B.B. shouted, and began stoking up the furnace. 'Into the Drop!'

Thrax looked at the wooden crate. 'There's Barny Juno's name written on here. And "Ladderland". Isn't that where he lives?'

'Never mind what's written on it, get rid of the damn thing and quick about it!' she shouted, cranking a black handle in blasts of steam. 'Yours not to reason why! Where's the sense in crowing about detail and duty! Just do it!'

'Eh?'

'Soften it up with a few kicks, then into the Drop! And the rest of that stuff!'

The Beast Man booted the crate a few times without inspiration, denting it in, then kicked it skidding into the Drop. It fell out of sight.

So this is the white-collar world, he thought, and remembered a saying of Violaine: 'Work keeps you occupied during the period of your life when you might be doing something useful.'

Sweeney was folded and compressed like a bloom packed in a bud. But now he found himself weightless and without direction, feeling something new which aged instantly. As he extended his many legs into a ghost-burnt vacuum, the crate fragments floating away from him, he looked into blasts of detergent like a recurring white sunset. Opinions, crumbs and insignificance slashed past his skull-cowling in a grey blizzard. He'd got off at the wrong end of the universe. This was a realm of results and grievances, gritty smithereens, the essence of the human world. Their vacuum was far superior to his, receding past zero into the negative. What he was feeling was boredom. 'We're downright colourful by comparison. At least we've got a sense of theatre.' He suddenly saw the answer with absolute clarity. 'We got it wrong . . . we're not the enemy. We just gathered another centre to ourselves.' He tried to breathe, falling away into the glint and scratch of empty noise.

The epicene demon Rammstein fretted in the cavern, pacing like a parrot. Sweeney had been gone too long and a stumped throne was wrong, wrong – something had thinned and broken.

The light changed, flensing his shadow into flickering feathers. He knelt, drained and feeble.

The colossal bleeding throne began to pulse, sprouting a set of massive blades. Spinning like a top, it unfolded a body of recurrences, snipping barbs and gripping hooks, spraying

125

sizzling blood like a Catherine wheel. It slowed, hissing, limbs still agitated, a morass of agonies heaving at its heart. Eyes slammed open in the black hull.

E.H. Hunt watched a jellyfish full of broken veins swim off into the chilling, darkening sea. Stars like thorns pushed through above as he prepared to cast off. But the crowd of animals which had joined Mister Braintree was no longer content to watch from the dissolving seawalls and had begun wandering aboard, settling in as though at home. 'This leopard is seemingly intent on carrying my trousers to the top of the sterncastle,' screamed Hunt to the Announcement Horse.

'Understandable,' chimed the iron steed, whose talent for inanimate pride now found full expression as the ship's figurehead. 'Since by your systematic theft you have created a floating replica of Ladderland.'

'Eh?'

'Where are you going, E.H. Hunt?' called Plantin Edge from the beach. He and Gregor had trolled up with some kind of battered whisky still.

'How obvious must something be before one's mother doesn't say it?'

'Beyond.'

'You have your answer. I hunt big births and terminal risks, strange stronger places and perhaps a whale with teeth as tall and hairy as a man. When they find recordings of my navigation sobs, they'll see the harrowing side. Did you ever think it'd be like this? Keep those bloody animals away from here!'

Another gaggle of wildlife was trailing toward the ramp. They were the circus animals, following their instinct for inconvenience. They tramped on deck and began scrapping with the others.

Hunt hauled on mast ropes and the sails opened, dislodging several chimps. Midnight faces covered the mainsail. 'Obviously drawn in a studio,' Edgy remarked.

'What?' Hunt called, exasperated, and cast off. A panther leapt on to his back, clinging on until the Fatal Rhino hooked it away with a snorting toss of its horn. The ramp fell into the surf as the tall boat moved. Hunt didn't have any buoys so he used orange spacehoppers, guylines tied to their antlers. The ship hauled out between these, the hull passing through the sky of an urchin sleeping transparent in coral. 'All these winged and stepping animals that have suddenly become a part of my life – the vessel won't take the weight!' And he dragged his treasure chest across the deck to the rail, unlatching the lid and tipping it over. A gush of sea water poured out, joining the ocean. Hunt was screaming, demented, phlegm dripping from his beard as the ship moved off, its equine figurehead prowing into the spray.

The vessel was a tower of tumbling biology. As its caterwauling noise receded into the dark, Edgy and Gregor watched from the shore. 'So all was justly appointed and no one was hurt,' said Edgy with satisfaction.

'How are we going to distribute these?' asked Gregor, holding a wad of leaflets which proclaimed EDGY'S STILL BY THE SEA. HE WAITS ON YOU WITH HOT LUBRICATION.

'By hand, I suppose,' Edgy muttered. 'Through people's doors? There's no other system. We'll get Barny to help us. A week to worry, another to pine, a third to know we've wasted our time.'

On the bluff behind them an angel landed, fragile as a feather made of bone. Under a sky deep as grief it closed its silent white wings.

Edgy turned. 'Mike?'

The angel blinked its black eyes. 'I like it here. As Violaine said: "Paradise is individually reflexive –"'

– *otherwise it might not be to everyone's taste.* I had once pulled up the truth-sentence like a buried rope from the sand, hadn't I? But interrupting favoured myths is a hazardous undertaking. The sidelines swallow honest men, removing all but their eyes.

Watching the tall man, the round man, the angel, I decide I've been witness to enough. Now I cast my own ashes over my shoulder and try my luck in the sky.

A patch of dark in the night, the place dwindles. Insane at last, blood flowing from a dream. Taking my every effort in a ghost of a head, I shoot the works. My mind melts into tears, and I can't remember the first line.